DEATH
with an Ocean View

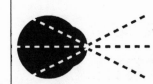This Large Print Book carries the
Seal of Approval of N.A.V.H.

DEATH
with an Ocean View

NORA
CHARLES

WHEELER
PUBLISHING

Published in 2004 by arrangement with The Berkley Publishing Group, a division of Penguin Group (USA) Inc.

Wheeler Large Print Cozy Mystery.

The text of this Large Print edition is unabridged.
Other aspects of the book may vary from the original edition.

Set in 16 pt. Plantin.

Printed in the United States on permanent paper.

Library of Congress Cataloging-in-Publication Data

Charles, Nora.
      Death with an ocean view / Nora Charles.
        p. cm.
      ISBN 1-58724-768-2 (lg. print : sc : alk. paper)
      1. Women detectives — Florida — Fiction.   2. Real estate development — Fiction.   3. Florida — Fiction.
      4. Large type books.   I. Title.
      PS3573.A42116D43 2004
      813'.6—dc22   2004052042

To Gloria and Paul Stuart

National Association for Visually Handicapped
---------------------- serving the partially seeing

As the Founder/CEO of NAVH, the only national health agency solely devoted to those who, although not totally blind, have an eye disease which could lead to serious visual impairment, I am pleased to recognize Thorndike Press* as one of the leading publishers in the large print field.

Founded in 1954 in San Francisco to prepare large print textbooks for partially seeing children, NAVH became the pioneer and standard setting agency in the preparation of large type.

Today, those publishers who meet our standards carry the prestigious "Seal of Approval" indicating high quality large print. We are delighted that Thorndike Press is one of the publishers whose titles meet these standards. We are also pleased to recognize the significant contribution Thorndike Press is making in this important and growing field.

Lorraine H. Marchi, L.H.D.
Founder/CEO
NAVH

* Thorndike Press encompasses the following imprints: Thorndike, Wheeler, Walker and Large Print Press.

ACKNOWLEDGMENTS

In Washington, D.C.

Thanks to Peggy Hanson for reading, editing, and suggesting, and allowing me to base Kate's Ballou on the Hansons' precious Ballou. And to Cordelia Benedict for listening, editing, and encouraging. And to the Rector Lane Irregulars: Carla Coupe, Ellen Crosby, Peggy Hanson, Valerie Patterson, Laura Weatherly, and Sandi Wilson. Special thanks to my Sunday morning walking pals: Dr. Diane Shrier for helping me understand Kate better and Pat Sanders for asking the right questions. And to Susan Kavanagh and Gail Prensky for listening and supporting.

In South Florida

Thanks to Gloria and Paul Stuart for keeping my room ready and for their excellent ongoing advice and counsel. Thanks to Diane and Dave Dufour for always being there. And to Joyce Sweeney's Writers' Workshop for critiquing the first synopsis.

In New York and New Jersey

Thanks to my I'll-listen-to-anything-friend, Doris Holland, and my son, Bill Reckdenwald, for cheering me along. And many thanks to my agent, Peter Rubie, and my editor, Tom Colgan, for believing I could do this.

ONE

"Charlie, what the hell am I doing in paradise?" Kate glanced up at a cotton ball cloud bouncing along in a cornflower blue sky, not expecting an answer. Charlie Kennedy, her husband, had dropped dead six months ago, still clutching the pen he'd used to close on their beachfront condo.

Ballou tugged on his leash. Knowing the Westie missed Charlie, too, she picked up speed, splashing surf over her bare feet, and sending sand flying.

Another perfect day in South Florida. A cliché Kate considered pure propaganda, perpetuated by snow birds and retirees, who'd left behind change of seasons, grandchildren, and decent public transportation, and now felt obliged to rave about the weather on a daily basis.

She was more than fed up with sunshine. Palmetto Beach's six straight days of clear skies and mid-80-degree weather, tempered by an ocean breeze, had seriously deepened her depression.

It was raining in New York City. And according to Al Roker, unseasonably cold for October. The frost on the pumpkin. God, how she wished she were up there.

But she couldn't go home. Charlie and she had sold her beloved house in Rockville Centre. Strangers lived there now. A mouthy financial planner, his rotund wife who favored Lycra leggings and peasant blouses, and two teenagers with multiple pierced body parts and wicked overbites. The new owners had painted the brick Tudor's front door and shutters shocking pink. Kate's former neighbors probably would never speak to her again.

Her current home — a third-floor beach-front apartment in the high-rise condo that had been Charlie's retirement choice, certainly not Kate's — was in danger of becoming a parking garage.

Exiting the Atlantic, a slim woman shouted, "Kate!" Stella Sajak, president of the Ocean Vista Condominium's Board of Directors, always sounded as if a crisis were coming and only she could stem its tide.

"Good morning, Stella." Kate, on the other hand, sounded priggish even to herself. A widow's voice? An invisible shield? A "don't you dare cross the line and feel sorry for me" voice?

"I hope we can count on you to support us at Town Hall this afternoon." Stella hopped on her left foot, tilted her head to the side, shook it, then pulled on her left ear. "Feels like half the ocean is in there. Damn, I

10

should have worn a bathing cap. But they're so old-lady-like, aren't they?"

Kate smiled, as one incipient old lady to another, but Stella missed — or ignored — the silent communication.

Ballou investigated a dead crab, then kicked it onto Kate's big toe.

"There's strength in numbers," Stella said. "We can't let that Sea Breeze bunch hoodwink the mayor and bamboozle our much too easily influenced city council. I'm telling you, those developers won't stop until they raze Ocean Vista, and leave us all homeless."

Then, giving her ear a final yank, she added, "It's your civic duty, Kate."

The wiry Stella, with blunt-cut steel gray hair, eyes of almost the same shade, and a nose that commanded notice, looked better in a bathing suit than most of Ocean Vista's residents. A daily dipper, she owned dozens of them. Today's choice, a crisp white eyelet with sunny yellow daisies, had a halter top and a jaunty skirt.

Kate, seedy in sweatpants and one of Charlie's old T-shirts, knew that her silver hair needed a shampoo and her legs hadn't been shaved in — she shuddered — since Charlie died. God, could that be possible?

Just to get away, she said, "I'll be there, Stella. Two. Right?"

Stella narrowed her eyes, then coolly appraised Kate from top to bottom, and sniffed.

"Right. I'll drive. Be in the lobby at one-thirty."

Outwitted, Kate veered south, pulling the indignant Ballou behind her, and headed back to the condo.

Nestled between fast-track Fort Lauderdale and nouveau-riche Boca Raton, the once sleepy village of Palmetto Beach had been plagued by progress. A glitzy resort complex, complete with an ice rink, would replace the old fishing pier and its weather-beaten restaurant and sand-strewn stores. And Sea Breeze Inc., the resort's management company, had petitioned the city council to exercise the right of eminent domain and, for the public good and Palmetto Beach's development, tear down Ocean Vista and build a parking garage.

According to Stella, no one understood why the mayor and council had sold the prime oceanfront property to Sea Breeze, especially since two other Broward County towns had spurned the company's offer, but only after accusations of attempted bribery.

Kate didn't give a damn what happened to Palmetto Beach. And if she did, she'd probably root for the development company. Then Ocean Vista would be razed, and she'd be forced to relocate. But where would she go?

Not to live with either of her sons, that was for sure. She couldn't picture Kevin's wife or Peter's partner gleefully racing around redecorating a guest room in anticipation of her arrival. And much as she loved the boys, that would never be an option.

Her own guest room in the stark white-on-white condo — Peter's partner, Edmund, a plastic surgeon by profession, but an interior designer by passion, had decorated it — was crammed with Charlie's stuff. Box after box of memories she couldn't bear to open.

Still annoyed that Stella Sajak had coerced her, Kate blew-dry her hair, shaved her legs, and dressed in tan slacks and a white cotton shirt. Looking at Charlie's picture on her art deco dressing table, she smiled. "Okay, I hear you. I'll put on lipstick, too." Then she said good-bye to a dejected Ballou.

Kate stepped out of the elevator and waved at Stella, dressed in a gray linen suit and pacing around a bronze urn filled with fake lilies.

The sea foam lobby was furnished with two overstuffed darker green chenille sofas and several cozy groupings of rattan tables and chairs. Potted plastic plants abounded. Dead center stood a life-size imitation alabaster statue of the Greek goddess Aphrodite, surrounded by a bevy of winged Cupids, mixing Greek and Roman myths in a no doubt unintended, but nevertheless real, salute to multiculturalism.

Stella strode over and nudged Kate with

her briefcase. "We're taking Marlene's car. She's double-parked with the engine running, so hurry up."

The front desk, backed by a wall of one hundred and fifty pigeonholes — one for each apartment — was manned by the miserable Miss Mitford, who treated the residents as if they were in sixth grade and slow learners. She'd been hired in 1970, when Ocean Vista opened and the realtors started bringing in potential buyers. In addition to being the keeper of the keys, rumor had it that Mitford was the keeper of the condo owners' secrets. And her inside information about their private lives had assured lifetime job security.

She nodded curtly as Stella and Kate passed by.

The circular driveway, edged with royal palms and sweet-smelling hibiscus, led to State Road A1A, known in Palmetto Beach as Ocean Boulevard. Marlene Friedman's 1958 white Caddy convertible blocked its north lane. Horns blared and curses and threats filled the air, as drivers swerved to get around her, only to be thwarted by the southbound traffic.

Marlene stuck her head, topped with a platinum blond wiglet teased into sausage curls, out the driver's window, and yelled, "Get over it, fellow!"

The object of her attention, who'd been

pressing his palm on the horn of his silver SUV, navigated around Marlene's left rear fin, only to go hood-to-hood with a yellow Rabbit heading south toward Fort Lauderdale.

Stella yanked open Marlene's front passenger door. "Get in, Kate, I'll ride in the back."

Before Kate could fasten her seat belt, Marlene pumped the gas pedal and they lurched forward. "Take it easy, Marlene! That guy's closing in behind us."

"Exactly why we're moving at eighty miles per. Can't you see that SOB in the SUV is dangerous? And my horoscope said death would visit today."

Stella groaned. "It's Halloween. The eve of All Souls' Day. Death, masquerading as costumed children, visits every Halloween. Of course, I never answer the door. That Key West fortune-teller certainly saw you coming. Fifty bucks thrown away."

"Madame X is an astrologer, not a fortune-teller, Stella. And your moon is in Taurus. So you'd better beware." Marlene made a sharp left onto Neptune Boulevard, heading for the bridge.

Marlene Friedman had been Kate Kennedy's best friend for almost sixty years, including a brief stint during the early seventies when she also had been Kate's sister-in-law. Marlene described her second marriage to Charlie's brother, Kevin, which had lasted less than six weeks, as a long date.

Twelve years ago, Marlene had buried her third husband, moved from Summit, New Jersey, to Palmetto Beach, and begun lobbying her former in-laws to "come on down."

After Charlie had retired from the force, he and Kate visited Marlene often. He loved beautiful beaches and challenging golf courses and Palmetto Beach had both.

Then six months ago, after debating for a decade about where to spend the rest of their lives, they finally moved. The rest of Charlie's life turned out to be less than twenty-four hours.

Not unexpectedly, the Neptune Boulevard drawbridge was rising. Kate couldn't recall ever having crossed over to the mainland without waiting.

In the backseat, Stella squirmed. "Damn, we'll be late!"

But today, Kate, who usually ignored Palmetto Beach's considerable charm, welcomed the delay, savoring the beauty of the dark blue water shimmering under the bright sunshine, and watching as a huge sloop and several powerboats, flanked by the mansions on both shores, lined up to sail under the bridge.

A thump on the Caddy's rear bumper startled Kate. She turned and spotted the silver SUV just as Stella, adjusting her glasses, peered out the back window, and said, "My God, David Fry is driving that gas guzzler."

16

"Who's David Fry?"

"Sea Breeze's CEO." Stella spun around and stared at Kate. "I can't believe you're so cavalier about Ocean View's future. Scandal and deception are the hallmarks of David Fry and his company. I believe that man bribed someone on the city council. He's the reason why we're fighting Town Hall."

A tiny ghoul, maybe ten years old, appeared out of nowhere, holding a small Neiman Marcus shopping bag, and tapping on the front passenger window. Kate rolled it down.

"Happy Halloween." The sweet voice belonged to a girl, though the ghastly death mask and ghoul costume completely hid her gender. "My mother says taking candy from strangers is dangerous and I'm on a low-fat diet anyway, so money will be fine."

Marlene laughed, her deep, rumbling, straight-from-the-belly laugh that Kate knew so well, and said, "Only in South Florida."

The kid opened her shopping bag, filled to the brim with dollar bills, and stuck out her hand. "Trick or treat."

TWO

"Over my dead body!" Stella Sajak's shout silenced the rowdy standing-room-only crowd at Palmetto Beach's Town Hall, a feat that the mayor and her gavel had not been able to accomplish. Kate, leaning against the faux cherry wood wall, wedged between Stella and Marlene and directly across the auditorium from David Fry, jumped as she caught the handsome, white-haired Sea Breeze CEO glaring at the condo president. If looks could kill, Stella would be a goner.

Yet Kate said nothing.

She used to be a Chatty Cathy, except no one needed a string to get her started. When she graduated from grade school, she'd been voted "Most Talkative," and for the next half-century she'd never had trouble finding her voice . . . until last spring when Charlie died and suddenly she had nothing to say, except for conversations with a dead man.

Marlene had been eyeing Fry ever since they'd arrived. Let her tell Stella.

The meeting had started out mean, and was moving rapidly toward mob mentality. David Fry, at first cool and calm, had presented Sea Breeze's eminent domain case,

18

but the boos and shouts from the audience quickly drove him into a corner.

The mayor, an attractive blonde, somewhere in her sixties and dressed in an Armani suit — just how high a salary was Palmetto Beach paying Brenda Walters? — had tried to restore order, but her seemingly conciliatory tone toward Sea Breeze's request had triggered Stella's angry response.

Kate felt a poke in her ribs as Marlene whispered, "Fry's an attorney, you know. And a bachelor to boot. Beaucoup bucks. That yellow mansion right across the Intercoastal from Houston's is his. Lives there all alone. A real hunk, isn't he?"

Marlene, who knew the stats on every available South Florida male between sixty and death, must have missed Fry's killer look. And apparently, she hadn't noticed the unruly constituency.

The fattest of the three councilmen called for order, but the crowd shouted him down.

With mayhem moments away, the mayor banged the gavel and adjourned the meeting, assuring all that she'd reschedule another before the council voted.

As Kate, Marlene, and Stella made their way out, a breathless Mayor Walters dashed up to them, extending her hand to Stella. "We have a difference of opinion, but I promise you a fair hearing. And if you'd like, we can meet privately tomorrow morning."

Stanley Ferris, another of the condo owners, a retired dentist and practicing phi-landerer, wizened and weather-beaten, squeezed in between Marlene and Stella, draping a skinny arm around each of them.

"You ought to take our lovely mayor up on that invite, Stella."

Scowling, Stella shoved Stanley's elbow off her shoulder, just as an unruffled David Fry emerged from the crowd. A now visibly rat-tled Stella stumbled over her words while in-troducing the mayor as "B-B . . . Brenda" to Marlene, Stanley, and Kate. Fry, standing off to the side, appeared amused, almost smirking. Then, much to Kate's surprise, Stella, regaining her composure, smiled brightly at the mayor and said, "A condo president lives in hope of negotiation. I'll be in your office at eight."

The mayor laughed. A charming tinkle. "I'll be there at ten."

On their way home, Stella sounded almost optimistic. "The mayor's first term is up next year. Says she won't run again, but they all say that; she's campaigning already. And after today's fiasco, you can bet that Brenda Walters has to be rethinking Sea Breeze's offer."

Marlene groaned. "Enough! If the bad guys win and David Fry buys us out, I'm heading north. You meet a better class of crooks in Palm Beach."

The giggle that rose in Kate's throat escaped like an uncontrollable hiccup, startling her.

Marlene managed to check on a crack in her bright orange acrylic thumbnail while making a left turn. "Let's talk about something fun — like tonight's party." She glanced over her shoulder and met Kate's eyes. "I'm going as Britney Spears, but I just happen to have a serving wench's costume in storage. If we turned up the hem, made a few nips and tucks, and bought a well-padded push-up bra, you could wear it."

Feeling her face flush, Kate pulled away from Marlene's gaze and stared out the window.

"For God's sake, Marlene," Stella said, "forget your nails, shut up about Halloween, and watch the road."

Marlene smirked, but faced forward. She slowed down as she approached the Intercoastal, and the drawbridge, as if on cue, went up.

This time Kate laughed out loud.

Once on the island, Marlene stopped to buy a *Sun-Sentinel* from one of the newsboys — men, actually, and mostly homeless — stationed on the corner of Neptune Boulevard and A1A. This one they knew by name. Timmy. Every day, he stood in the blazing sun from seven until four. And early mornings were tough for Timmy — he'd told Marlene that he had trouble getting started. He wore a bright pink T-shirt, with the newspaper's logo spread across its front, dirty cutoffs, and a tan that had turned muddy decades ago. Thanking Marlene for the dollar and the "keep the change," he smiled, exuding a raffish charm. But today, Timmy's right front tooth was missing. Kate felt a pang and feared unbidden tears would flow.

These "newsboys" sporting *Sun-Sentinel* pink or *Miami Herald* blue T-shirts criss-crossed all the main intersections of Broward County. Kate thought of them as the walking wounded, and if Charlie hadn't gone and died on her, she would have volunteered at a homeless shelter. God, that logic made no sense, even to her. She pulled a tissue out of her purse and blew her nose. Could she be losing it?

In the lobby, piped-in Frank Sinatra singing "High Hopes" drowned out the fountain's noisy gurgle.

Miss Mitford, a wispy strand of white hair escaping her bun, but doing nothing to soften her stern demeanor, waved Stella over to the desk. "You have a letter, Mrs. Sajak. Hand delivered."

Good-quality ecru linen paper, Kate thought, like a formal wedding invitation. Or at least, the way wedding invitations used to look before they started arriving in odd-shaped envelopes and in every color of the rainbow.

Stella stared at the envelope in silence, then shoved it into her briefcase and said, "I'll see you tonight, Marlene. Good-bye Kate. You really should consider coming to the Halloween party. I'm going as Carrie Nation. Complete in every detail. I'm even carrying an ax." Then she spun around, strode back across the lobby, and went out the front door.

Having changed into sweatpants and another of Charlie's T-shirts, Kate stood at the kitchen counter and dined directly from the refrigerator. A peanut butter and jelly sandwich on whole wheat and a Hershey's Chocolate ice cream Dixie Cup. Unless microwaving a Lean Cuisine or hard-boiling an egg counted as cooking, Kate hadn't fixed a real meal since Charlie died.

Ballou fared better, lapping up the last of the casserole that Marlene had dropped off last night.

An excellent and adventurous chef, Marlene frequently delivered home-cooked dinners and usually hung around to make sure that Kate and Ballou ate them. Ballou, like most males, adored Marlene, who'd spoiled him since puppyhood. As much as Kate appreciated Marlene's ongoing acts of kindness, she also resented her swooping in uninvited and parking herself in front of the television to watch god-awful trash like *Fear Factor*.

No worry about that tonight. Marlene, after a last-ditch effort to talk Kate into coming to the Halloween party, went home to "turn myself into Britney." That would require quite a transformation, Kate thought as she licked the last of her ice cream off the spoon.

"Well, Ballou, I guess what I've turned into is a bitch. Let's go for a walk on the beach."

Moon over Miami had nothing over sunset on Palmetto Beach's horizon. The sky, now streaked with vivid shades of blue, gold, and orange, was slowly muting into navy blue. Soon a harvest moon would hang in the heavens, shining down on the ocean and bathing the beach with its light.

They walked for almost an hour, past the pier, where older, pale green, dusty coral, and soft beige condominiums lined the beachfront, all the way to the lighthouse. Then, reluctantly, she started back home.

A scarecrow aimed a video camera, as assorted ghouls, goblins, witches, and an aging Elvis paraded around the pool and across the patio and entered the recreation room via the double glass doors. Kate crouched behind a scruffy brush of sea grape, soothed a nervous Ballou, and watched the action.

Stella, as promised, carried an ax and looked angry. In character as Carrie Nation? Or in character as Sajak the crusader?

Marlene's very much in evidence bare midriff made Kate gasp. If the committee was awarding a prize for the most audacious costume, her former sister-in-law had it all sewn up.

Hours later, Kate stood on her balcony under the light of that full moon, listening to the music and the sounds of laughter drifting up from the rec room, holding Ballou, and feeling sorry for herself. Actually, the only thing she savored these lonely nights was self-pity.

Stanley Ferris, dressed in a Texas Ranger costume, appeared on the patio, then almost ran around the pool, checking over his shoulder. Could the silly old goat be heading to the beach for a midnight assignation?

Based on his womanizing reputation and his rumored overdosing on Viagra, that would be Kate's guess.

Stanley shed his snakeskin boots and ten-gallon hat. No doubt in anticipation of some septuagenarian *From Here to Eternity* sex in the surf. For the second time that day, Kate laughed aloud. Then Stanley stumbled over something spread across what appeared to be a previously laid blanket.

A figure, approaching from the right, caught Kate's eye.

Mary Frances Costello, Broward County's reigning Tango Champion, yoga student, and ex-nun, made her way through the sand, seriously hampered by her Scarlett O'Hara hoop skirt. Just as Mary Frances reached the blanket, Stanley yelled, "Stella!" then collapsed.

Mary Frances's shrieks drowned out the Ocean Vista band's rendition of "Strangers in the Night."

Kate put a frantically barking Ballou down, dashed inside to the phone, and dialed 911.

THREE

The Palmetto Beach Police, sirens blaring, arrived at Ocean Vista a little after midnight. Kate was questioned by Detective Nick Carbone, a surly, dark, balding, middle-aged man, losing the battle of the bulge above his low-slung belt and, seemingly, suspicious of her every word. He left her apartment at twelve thirty-five with a curt, "We'll need to take a full statement. Be at the police station tomorrow afternoon at four. I'll meet you at the front desk."

Kate couldn't sleep. The Stanley-Stella beach scene played over and over in her mind, like a movie without an end.

At a quarter to one, restless, she paced the small balcony, Ballou at her side, and watched the last of the still-costumed condo owners straggle out of the rec room, wondering if the cops who'd questioned them had been as intense and suspicious as Carbone.

Stanley Ferris, wearing his Texas ranger hat but walking like the little old man he was, followed a uniformed cop around to the right of the building. Heading to Stanley's car? To a patrol car? At least they hadn't handcuffed

27

him. Kate sighed and looked toward the ocean. A crime team had set up spotlights in the sand and were wrapping yellow tape around the blanket. The full moon that she'd admired earlier in the evening now appeared to glare at her. Garish. Obtrusive. God how she missed Charlie!

After a long night and an early morning walk with Ballou, Kate, wearing a floppy straw hat and smeared head-to-toe with 40-block sunscreen, collapsed into a beach chair under a yellow and white umbrella at the pool. She couldn't concentrate on the *Sun-Sentinel*'s crossword puzzle, because something that had happened yesterday at the Town Hall now eluded her. Something about Stella. Something odd. But what? How she hated these senior moments.

"Well, I guess someone took Stella's 'over my dead body' literally." Marlene lowered her considerable girth onto the chaise next to Kate.

No block, straw hat, or umbrella for Marlene. Only a red tankini protected her from the midday sun. Her creased skin, the color of lightly toasted whole wheat, and her aqua-shadowed lids provided a startling contrast to her platinum hair swept up into a French twist. Marlene, never seen without full eye makeup — even when swimming — could still jackknife and backstroke like a teenager.

Kate put down her pen, turned to her former sister-in-law, and managed to force a smile, noting that Marlene's attempt to reciprocate looked more like a grimace. "Is Stanley in jail?"

"The last I saw of our sleazy septuagenarian, a cop was growling at him."

"You don't think he killed Stella, do you?"

Marlene shook her head. "You know, sometimes I felt like killing Stella myself. She cheated at Hearts. I wound up with the Queen of Spades in every hand that woman dealt. Anyway, now that she's dead, we'll need a fourth." Suddenly a smile brightened Marlene's face. "Why don't you take her place in our lonely Hearts game? Of course, we won't play again until after the funeral."

"I hardly knew her. What was she like?"

"Something of a mystery. And apparently, a liar, too."

"If only I'd warned Stella about David Fry's killer look during the Town Hall meeting. Or called 911 sooner. Of course, as I told that extremely unpleasant Detective Carbone, Stella had been long dead by the time I saw Stanley stumble over her body. Dear Lord! Shot through the back of the head." Kate shivered in the sunshine, then asked, "Why was she a mystery? And a liar?"

"Well, did you know that I'm her executrix?"

Kate didn't.

"And lots of things don't add up. I spent

29

all morning calling the list of people that she wanted invited to her funeral. She'd told me that Pat Sajak and her dead husband were first cousins. So I called *Wheel of Fortune*. Pat actually came to the phone. Said he never heard of Stella or her husband."

Marlene paused to take a sip from her ever-present can of Coke, as always, liberally laced with rum. Kate waved away her offer to share. "Go on."

"Then Stella asked Nancy Cooper, the society editor at the *Palmetto Beach Gazette*, to write her obituary. You know Nancy, she's way younger than most of us, lives in Penthouse Two, the one facing both the ocean and Fort Lauderdale's skyline. Anyhoo, I have a copy of the obit, so I called Northwestern, where Stella supposedly graduated cum laude in 1960, to let them know. For their alumni records. They never heard of her either."

Kate sneezed. She'd like to uproot then strangle that sweet-smelling, sneeze-inducing jasmine. "Strange. Have you ever met her husband?"

"Bless you." Marlene yanked a tissue out from her tankini top and handed it to Kate. "He died before Stella moved down here from Chicago ten years ago. No kids. Never had any company. Yet she thrived on being with people, loved the limelight, worked part-time for the Chamber of Commerce, and was

30

very active in local politics and in the condo, too."

Why would a Northwestern grad need a society editor to write her obituary? And why would this Nancy Cooper have agreed to do that? The *Palmetto Beach Gazette* had an excellent full-time obit writer on staff. Lots of dying went on in this town. Kate, like many of its residents, turned to the obituary page first. And why had no one from up North ever come to visit Stella?

Even though Kate had been here only six months, her older son, Kevin, a busy Flatbush firefighter, along with his wife, Jennifer, an even busier bond trader, and her youngest son, Peter, a not-so-busy freelance writer, and Edmund, the doctor/interior designer, had all visited twice since Charlie died. Her two granddaughters, one in college in Boston and the other a senior in high school, apparently the busiest of the bunch, had come down only for the funeral.

Stella Sajak had seemed too strident, too outgoing, too on-stage to be a mystery woman. But Kate had read enough of Carl Hiaasen to know that South Florida was a mecca for scalawags, swindlers, and scam artists. Former drug dealers lived in mansions on the Intercoastal. White-collar criminals, after serving time in country club prisons, changed their names, moved to Harbor Isle or Hobe Sound, then sailed into their sunset years, endowing libraries and hosting charity balls, without their neighbors ever suspecting that they once had been convicts.

"Here comes the dancing nun." Marlene's words pulled Kate out of speculation and back to reality.

Mary Frances Costello made her way through the maze of chaises and chairs, clearly heading in their direction. Kate had decided that there were two kinds of ex-nuns: Those who dressed in uniforms — not unlike their former habits — navy or gray polyester suits and white or cream blouses. And those who, wanting to make up for all the fashion fads they'd missed while living in the convent, dressed trendier than any teenager. Mary Frances, wearing a white halter and bell bottoms, fell into the latter category.

When she'd moved south from Minneapolis six years ago, Mary Frances had segued straight from the convent to the condo. Marlene, who in addition to knowing the stats on South Florida's over-sixty single men and keeping a mental dossier on Ocean Vista's owners, had told Kate that she found the pretty redhead to be among the most intriguing.

What Kate found particularly fascinating were Mary Frances's upper arms. Firm, muscular, yet feminine. No old lady bat wings waving in the wind. Could yoga be the reason why this gal could get away with —

well *almost* get away with — a halter?

Marlene had also told Kate, "Mary Frances lowers her age by a year every time anyone asks how old she is. Using her math, she must have become a nun in nursery school."

Svelte of figure and firm of face, with thick hair, big blue eyes, and a pug nose, Mary Frances could have passed for fifty, but Marlene had assured Kate that the ex-nun was over sixty.

Whatever her age, this morning, wiping her eyes and minus her makeup, Mary Frances looked great.

"Hey," Marlene shouted, "is Stanley in the hoosegow?"

Mary Frances wrinkled her nose in Marlene's direction as if she smelled something rotten. "You should be ashamed of yourself, Marlene, taking pleasure in the misfortune of others. I'm *so* sorry to disappoint you, but Stanley's upstairs sleeping."

"I figure he'd been booked, fingerprinted, and photographed. Is he out on bail?" Marlene spoke with relish, but patted the cushion on the chaise next to her, motioning for Mary Frances to sit down.

"You're a wicked woman." Mary Frances flicked her auburn curls from one shoulder to the other. "I have nothing to say to you."

"Now don't go getting your rosary beads in a twist. If you really don't believe that Stanley killed Stella, sit down and let's try to figure out who did."

To Kate's surprise, Mary Frances sat.

Marlene riffled through her airplane-carry-on-size tote — tomato red to match her tankini — and pulled a can of Coke out of a tiny cooler, then continued rummaging. "I have rum in here somewhere. Want me to add a shot?"

"God, no." Mary Frances sighed. "I had more than enough rum last night. My head aches and I can't even remember what I told that detective . . ."

"Carbone?" Kate asked before Marlene could open her mouth. "Kind of bulky and burly?"

"No." Mary Frances frowned. "Farber, I think. Short and skinny. Looked a little like Stanley. I kept getting them confused." She pressed the Coke can to her forehead. "I swear I'm never going to drink again."

"You didn't kill Stella, did you?" Marlene asked, holding up the bottle of rum. "You know, in a blackout?"

Mary Frances, in one fluid, graceful movement, stood up, then slowly walked to the back of Marlene's chaise and poured the entire can of Coke over her head.

FOUR

Kate watched Marlene step away from the outdoor shower at the deep end of the pool, and wrap a white terry cloth turban around her just-rinsed hair. She wasn't surprised that her former sister-in-law had responded to the unexpected Coke shampoo with a veneer of good humor. Yet Kate sensed hostility. She'd watched Marlene cover up hurt feelings since first grade.

Back on the chaise, Marlene nodded in acknowledgment of Mary Frances's third apology. "I swear I don't know what in the world possessed me to do such a thing."

Grabbing a cosmetic case from the zippered pocket in Marlene's tote bag, Kate handed it to her.

Marlene pulled out a mirror, and surveyed the damage. "Yuck. You really did a job on my mascara, Mary Frances. Ran right down into my puppet lines. A new wrinkle in makeup. Charcoal gray streaks to highlight our deepest creases. I'm going to market the idea to Max Factor."

Mary Frances's blush started at the base of her neck and quickly spread to her forehead. "Please let me take you and Kate to lunch. A small way to show you how sorry I am for my childish behavior. Besides, I desperately need to talk to you both about the murder. About Stanley and" — she sighed and turned an even darker red — "Stella."

Kate knew Mary Frances's fourth apology was a winner. With an invitation like that, Marlene would have dined with the devil himself.

The Ocean Vista's dining room, all cheery blue and white checks with white Formica tables and chairs, usually noisy and bustling at high noon, was subdued. Far fewer people eating lunch today. And those who were wore funeral faces. Kate questioned their sincerity, but realized that judgment was based on what Marlene believed and had repeated again this morning, "Most of the condo owners thought Stella was a tyrant. And most, except for a few foolish old women, consider Stanley a snake." Could Stella's murder and Stanley's being the prime suspect have changed their neighbors' opinions overnight? Or had Marlene been wrong?

The sun streaming in through the window streaked the daily choices. Kate shifted her chair, so she could read the menu. Across from her, Marlene had decided.

"I'll have the flounder," she was telling the perky blond waitress, whose hand-written name tag read TIFFANI — with a red heart drawn over the I — and who wore neon green high heel sneakers and a megawatt smile.

Tiffani nodded approvingly. "It's fresh caught this morning. I heard the chef say, 'At least the fish won't kill anyone today.'"

With that assurance, Kate ordered the flounder, too.

Mary Frances opted for scrambled eggs and dry toast.

Nursing an upset stomach or on a diet? She certainly didn't look ill, but maybe . . .

"Tiffani!" Marlene called after the waitress. "A bottle of dry white wine would be nice. And you can bring me a Caesar salad, too. And a hot fudge sundae for dessert. Miss Costello's paying."

Mary Frances's fifth apology mercifully ended when Tiffani brought the food. Marlene dug right in.

Sipping her tea and playing with her eggs, Mary Frances frowned. "I need some advice, but I want you both to promise to keep what I'm about to say confidential."

Marlene drained her white wine, then raised her right hand. "I'll keep it as sacred and as secret as the seal of the confessional."

"It's not the penitent," Kate said, "it's the priest who's bound to secrecy."

"Don't be so technical. The point is I will never reveal what Mary Frances tells us, not even under torture."

A slight smile formed, then faded on Mary Frances's face. "For some strange reason, I believe Marlene. Or maybe I'm just so desperate." She started to cry. Loud sobs, accompanied by heaving shoulders.

Kate patted her arm. "What is it?"

"Stanley may have murdered Stella." Mary Frances used her napkin to wipe her eyes.

"But you said . . ." Marlene started.

Under the table, Kate kicked Marlene's shin, then turned to Mary Frances. Using her most motherly tone, she said, "Tell us why you think that."

"Well, first off, he's vice-president of the condo association. I know for a fact that he coveted Stella's job."

"Good God, woman," Marlene spat out the words. "You don't really believe that Stanley would kill Stella to become condo president, do you?"

Mary Frances stared at her cold eggs.

"There's something else, isn't there?" Kate asked gently.

Mary Frances nodded. "Stanley left the Halloween party, well before his scheduled rendezvous with me. Stella ducked out a few minutes later. When he returned, alone, I watched him, standing on the patio, dumping sand out of these snakeskin boots." She almost hissed the last few words.

A woman scorned? Kate wondered.

Mary Frances hadn't finished. "Stella never

came back. The next time I saw her, she was dead."

Marlene, moving her chair out of Kate's range, said, "Did you ask Stanley where he'd gone?"

"I didn't have to ask. He'd spent a good part of the evening huddled in private conversations with Stella. That's probably why I drank so much. I even overheard Stella, bold as brass, flirting with him. It almost sounded as if she'd had an affair with him."

"Certainly does!" Marlene said, almost gleefully. "So he went down to the beach, laid the blanket, waited for Stella to arrive, shot her, went back to the party, then later returned to the scene of the crime to meet you."

Kate shook her head. "We don't know that happened." Kate had heard Stanley scream, "Stella!" She remembered the horror in his voice.

Mary Frances shoved her eggs to one side, and said, "Indeed, we don't. Lots of people went out on the patio for a smoke or a smooch or a whiff of ocean air. For example, Marlene, you left the party around the same time as Stella, but you came back as alive and annoying as ever."

"For God's sake," Marlene shouted, "don't change your suspect in mid-sentence. Stella was found dead on Stanley's blanket, wasn't she?" Marlene pointed a finger, its orange nail glittering in the sunshine, in Mary Frances's direction. "And you didn't tell the police what you'd overheard, did you?"

"No." Mary Frances started sobbing again, then jumped up, and fled from the dining room.

"Damn that woman!" Marlene said. "She ran off and stuck us with the check."

"I have to get ready for my interview with Detective Carbone." Kate placed a twenty-dollar bill on the table and started to stand up. "Good Lord, isn't that David Fry?" She froze, suddenly overcome by irrational fear. She had no doubt that Fry wanted Stella silenced, but he wouldn't have permanently shut her up, would he?

"Where?"

"He just walked through the door with a woman I know, but can't place. They're heading in our direction."

Marlene whipped her neck around so fast that Kate could hear it crack.

"Of all the gin joints in the world, he walks into Ocean Vista's dining room on the day my hair is hidden under a turban and my makeup is messed up beyond repair."

Kate willed herself to calm down. "Who's the blonde?"

"Nancy Cooper. The society editor for the *Gazette*. We just talked about her earlier. How can you have lived here for six months, so insulated and isolated that you don't recognize your neighbors?"

"I've seen her in the lobby; I just couldn't put a name to the face. And she can't be more than forty or forty-five. Rather young to be living in Ocean Vista, isn't she?"

"Do sit down, Kate. They're almost here. God, he's gorgeous. So Cary Grant. But why is Nancy consorting with the enemy? Not that I'd be above a little consorting myself."

"Hello, Marlene." Nancy's deep voice sounded somber. "Have you ladies met David Fry?" Not waiting for Marlene to answer, Nancy turned to Kate, extending a hand. "I'm Nancy Cooper. You're the widow in 301, right?"

Was that to be her new identity? Where had Kate, the girl with the chestnut curls, gone? Kate, the airline stewardess? Kate, the wife? Kate, the mother? Kate, the grand-mother? Would she forever more be defined by Charlie's death?

She stood, shaky, afraid she might scream. "The name is Kennedy. Kate Kennedy. Please excuse me. I have an appointment."

Twenty minutes later, out of the shower and deciding what to wear to her interview with Detective Carbone, Kate heard Marlene's distinctive rat-a-tat-tat on her door. Ballou barked energetically, welcoming her.

She hesitated, then opened it. "Sorry. I don't have time to talk."

41

"We have to talk. You don't have to be at the police station till four. It's only two-thirty. Sit down." Marlene motioned toward the living room. "This won't take long."

Kate sighed, then retied her white terry cloth robe, and led Marlene, who was being licked by an adoring Ballou, through the foyer to the off-white couch. She sat on the edge of a taupe wing chair. "I have things to do before I leave. You have five minutes."

"Look, Nancy Cooper may be shallow, but she isn't cruel. Just doesn't think. Wait till you see how she plays Hearts. You'll cream her. So she didn't know your name. Hell, you didn't know hers either."

"Was my running away that obvious?"

"Absolutely." Behind Marlene's bravado, Kate sensed anxiety.

Kate's stomach knotted. Acid gurgled. The truth hurt. She said nothing, wondering if Marlene could hear the rumbling. But the rest of her body language remained as still as the silence, and though ashamed to admit it, Kate rather enjoyed watching Marlene squirm.

In these standoffs — they'd never had a real quarrel — Marlene had always been the one to speak first.

After an eternity of seconds, Marlene waved her right arm. "Maybe people see you as a widow because that's the role you've chosen to play. You see yourself as Charlie's widow, so why are you surprised when that's the way the world reacts to you?"

The acid rose up and almost gagged Kate.

"Listen to me, Kate" — the tremble in Marlene's voice confirmed her nervousness — "you and I should try to figure out who killed Stella."

Where had *that* come from? Her old friend never ceased to amaze.

Marlene was now talking with both hands. "Despite my tormenting Mary Frances, I don't think Stanley Ferris has the moxie to murder a moth. The motive must be connected to Stella's mysterious past. And who knows how many of Palmetto Beach's residents aren't who or what they say they are."

Kate had been thinking about that, too. And about David Fry. And about trying to dredge up whatever it was that she couldn't remember about the Town Hall meeting. It had happened as they were leaving. Stanley had draped one arm over Marlene's shoulders and another over Stella's, just before the mayor had agreed to talk to Stella the next morning. David Fry had been standing close by, smirking at them. Would that meeting with Stella have changed the mayor's mind? Leaving David Fry and Sea Breeze out in the cold? And hadn't Mary Frances been there? Right behind Stanley? Did that mean anything? Kate again reached in vain for the missing piece of the puzzle.

Annoying. But at least she felt better.

"Is this just another scheme to take my mind off Charlie?"

"Hell, no." Marlene's voice sounded steadier. "We need to remember everything he said. Charlie Kennedy was the best damn homicide detective in New York City. Didn't he tell us so a million times? With all those murder cases we've heard about and all those Agatha Christie mysteries we've read, we're probably better prepared for the job than the Palmetto Beach Police Department. Nothing like becoming embroiled in a good murder to take your mind off grief . . ." Marlene suddenly shut up, as if worried that she'd gone too far.

Kate had read a shelf load of books dealing with the grieving process. She knew that to assuage their grief, some widows took on the identity of their late husbands. She'd suspected she was one of them. While working on a homicide, Charlie had shared his theories with her. And she'd saved all his case files. It might be like having him around again.

"You know, Marlene, perhaps we could ask a few discreet questions."

FIVE

Resentment and remembrance, a deadly combination, ate away at her psyche.

Marlene frowned at her cold-cream-covered reflection in the mirror, then rigorously removed the streaked makeup. Too bad secrets and lies and their by-products, guilt and fear, couldn't be wiped away with a Kleenex.

God knows if she could erase the slate, she would — but she couldn't, and neither worry nor regret would change a damn thing.

Marlene sighed, then rinsed her face, patted it dry, and applied astringent, forcing herself to concentrate on the task at hand, putting on a new face.

Hell, she'd just have to go on living with her stained soul.

As she reached for the eyelash curler, the phone rang.

Naked, she navigated around the clothes and shoes strewn across the bedroom and picked up her aqua Princess Phone. A treasure she'd hung on to through three husbands.

"Marlene Friedman." She'd also hung on to her maiden name.

"Miz Friedman, this is Mr. Adams, of the Adams Family Mortuary." He spoke with a

45

thick Southern accent and in a mournful monotone. "I'd like to meet with you as soon as possible to go over the late Stella Sajak's funeral arrangements."

"What? With me?"

"Yes, ma'am. Miz Sajak's attorney just called. The police expect to have the autopsy completed by late tomorrow, then they'll release the body to us either tomorrow evening or early Friday morning. And, well, ma'am, since you're the deceased's executrix, you'll be the one in charge."

Marlene picked up a pink marabou slipper lying on the table next to the phone, and flung it across the room. "I wasn't aware that Stella's funeral would be my responsibility, Mr. — er — Adams."

"Oh yes, ma'am, the attorney has assured me that you're the designated planner. You have a budget of ten thousand dollars. We can arrange a mighty fine memorial service. Could you come by early this evening? Say five-thirty. We're between viewings then."

"Certainly, Mr. Adams. There's nothing I'd rather be doing at cocktail hour than picking out a coffin."

She hung up and called Kate. "Let's make a deal. I'll drive you to the police station, if you'll come with me to the funeral parlor."

Marlene riffled through her closet, and finally found her grape and plum chiffon jumpsuit hidden under a yellow duster. The

46

plum in the floral print was an exact match for her lipstick. She stepped into plum wedgies and added an amethyst necklace and matching bracelet. Placing a 45 record on the turntable, she checked herself in a full-length mirror.

Not bad for a fat old lady with a checkered past.

The smooth strains of "The Stars Fell on Alabama" filled the bedroom. This time the memories felt good. August '57. Cotton candy. Kernels from sweet corn on the cob stuck in her teeth. Screaming on Playland's roller coaster. Betting on penny-ante poker in the arcade. French-kissing under the board-walk. Marlene had jump-started the hippies' summer of love by more than a decade.

She was smiling when she arrived in the lobby.

Kate, wearing khaki pants, a blue button-down, cotton shirt, and brown loafers — not very different from the classic look she favored in high school — stood at the front desk, chatting with the dour Miss Mitford. Marlene noted with satisfaction that Kate had taken the time to apply makeup and blow-dry her thick silver hair.

"I've been asking Miss Mitford about the note that Stella received yesterday."

Score one for Kate. Marlene had forgotten all about that. "And?"

"Timmy hand-delivered it, while we were

at the Town Hall meeting."

"Timmy? You mean my Timmy, who sells the *Sun-Sentinel* on Neptune Boulevard and A1A?"

"Yes. Miss Mitford described him perfectly."

Pride flickered on the desk clerk's sourpuss. By God, Kate had charmed the dragon lady.

"Said he was only the delivery boy." Miss Mitford sounded less miserable than usual. "Someone must have paid him to bring it here. I hope he used the money for a bath. Smelled like a skunk. I'd just finished spraying disinfectant when Mrs. Sajak and you two ladies returned."

"Thank you, again." Kate, her green eyes glowing, turned from the desk and said, "Come on, Marlene, it's only three-thirty, let's go find Timmy."

With the top down, the sun warmed their faces, and the ocean breeze ruffled Kate's hair, but Marlene knew her teased twist was weatherproof.

On the approach to the bridge, the *Miami Herald* newsboy — like Timmy, well into middle age and tanned to the color of tobacco — worked both sides of the road, darting back and forth to catch the incoming and outgoing cars.

Marlene leaned across Kate and yelled, "Paper!"

As the man weaved his way through the

traffic, Kate twisted around and glanced over her shoulder toward the ocean. "I don't see Timmy anywhere."

"And that's really odd," Marlene said. "A lot of these guys don't last a day, never mind a season. But this has been Timmy's turf for years. He's as dependable as the humidity."

The *Miami Herald* guy smiled, thrusting the paper at Kate. She handed him a dollar bill. "Keep the change."

"Thanks!"

As he started across the boulevard, Kate grabbed the tail of his T-shirt. "Please, I have a question."

He turned, his watery blue eyes unhappy. "Hey, I have other customers, lady!"

"I'll make it quick. Where's Timmy?"

"Don't know. He never showed up today."

"When did you see him last?"

A horn blew.

"That's two questions, lady."

"It's important." Kate sounded contrite and sincere. June Cleaver, with just the right touch of Jessica Fletcher. Marlene felt more than justified in having tempted Kate to play detective.

"Timmy was jumpy all yesterday morning, then he left for about fifteen minutes in the early afternoon. Said he had a job to do, and that he'd been paid some good money. He came back and worked till four, but he seemed twitchy, then didn't show today. I

49

don't mind. With no *Sun-Sentinel* competition, I sold twice as many *Herald*s."

Marlene, thinking about how she'd bought a paper from Timmy after he'd delivered the note, snapped, "Well, did Timmy tell you who hired him?"

The man readjusted his newspapers, shook his head, and dashed off in the direction of the still honking horn.

The bridge came down and locked in place, and when Marlene didn't move forward fast enough, the driver of the silver SUV that had pulled up behind her honked, too. She spun around to gesture that they were, finally, heading across. The driver, showing great teeth, smiled, then waved.

"Kate, is that Killer-Look Fry following us?"

The Palmetto Beach Police Department shared a parking lot with Town Hall. Beige stucco and box-shape architecture made for a truly ugly building.

Kate grimaced. "Town Hall looks almost graceful by default."

Still thinking about David Fry, Marlene nodded vaguely as they walked through the front door.

The waiting room could have belonged to a low-rent dentist. Pale green walls, cheap rattan furniture, and even by Marlene's lax housekeeping standards, grimy and gritty.

Seated at a metal desk, a handsome young African-American, in a well-pressed uniform, looked up and smiled, "How can I help you, ladies?"

"I'm Mrs. Kennedy. And this is my sister-in-law, Mrs. Friedman. I have an appointment with Detective Carbone." Marlene thought Kate sounded nervous. After all these years, she still had trouble knowing what was really going on with Kate, who — even as a kid — kept her feelings to herself.

The officer stood. "Follow me, please. Detective Carbone is waiting for you."

Marlene walked alongside Kate.

"Not you, ma'am. Please have a seat. Mrs. Kennedy shouldn't be too long."

Marlene sat. Her own feelings were crystal clear — annoyed that she wouldn't hear what Kate told the detective — annoyed and a little worried.

Soul searching for the second time in one afternoon — she vowed not to let this become a habit — she didn't realize that someone had come through the door, and she jumped when a deep voice said, "Good afternoon, Ms. Friedman. Marlene, if I may. What a pleasant surprise. I didn't think we'd meet again so soon and in, of all places, a police station."

David Fry. Damn, he had been following them.

Frazzled, she stared at him. The enemy.

The man who wanted to tear down her home. The man Kate thought might have murdered Stella. The most gorgeous man in South Florida. Smiling at her.

"Let me apologize for honking at you as the bridge opened. I had no idea that you and Mrs. Kennedy were in the car in front of me. I never like to reveal my short fuse to such lovely ladies. Especially those I would like to have join me for cocktails. After my appointment with Detective Farber, of course."

She always had a weakness for scoundrels and snakes.

At this stage of the game, would the great scorekeeper in the sky even bother to count one more sleaze play?

Batting her eyes, she accepted David Fry's offer and arranged to meet him after she and Kate left the funeral parlor.

"Since we can't set a definite time to rendezvous, why don't you and Mrs. Kennedy come directly to my home? Anytime between six-thirty and seven would be fine. And perhaps I can entice you both to stay for dinner at eight."

Said the spider to the fly . . .

"That would be lovely," Marlene said, transfixed by his blue eyes and not yet frantic about how the hell she could explain this to Kate.

SIX

Detective Carbone picked at a hangnail on his left index finger. Kate's eyes moved from that distasteful operation to the name plate on his cluttered metal desk. NICHOLAS CARBONE. Had anyone ever called him Nicholas? Or Nicky? Probably not even his mother. He was definitely a Nick.

The room smelled from a half-eaten meatball hero, heavy on the garlic, lying on a stained paper napkin, next to a cup of black coffee, long gone cold. The air conditioner must have been set at 50 degrees. Kate pulled her navy blue cardigan out of her shoulder bag and slipped her right arm into a sleeve.

Carbone stopped picking and handed Kate a sheet of paper. "Your interview from last night. I typed it up right after I left you. Read it. See if anything jogs your memory. What you've told me so far hasn't been much help." With that, he raised his finger to his mouth.

God, was he going to bite off the hangnail? Kate turned away, pulling on her left sleeve and breathing deeply, not wanting to open her purse and pop a Pepcid AC. When she glanced at him again, he'd removed his finger from his mouth.

She squared her shoulders and swallowed hard. "There is something that I forgot to mention, but it has nothing to do with what I saw last night."

"And that would be?" His raspy voice reeked of skepticism.

"At the city council meeting yesterday afternoon, David Fry — you must know that he and Stella were involved in a nasty legal battle — anyway, as Stella argued her position, David Fry gave her a killer look."

Even to her ears, she sounded foolish.

"Is that right, Mrs. Kennedy? A killer look. I'll make a note of that. Now about Mr. Ferris's activities on Tuesday night."

"But I told you everything I witnessed."

"Just read the report. You might surprise both of us."

Embarrassed and flustered, she read. Carbone's detached writing style saddened her. A woman had been murdered on the beach, less than three yards from Kate's balcony. Had the words she'd chosen to describe that tragedy really been so dispassionate? Or had Carbone left out the passion for his own purposes?

Moving to the edge of her seat, Kate fought the urge to run, knowing she had to stay put until dismissed. "Yes, Detective Carbone. That's what I saw. It's what I felt that's missing."

"Okay, why don't we try again?"

Kate took it from the top. With more feeling, but no new facts.

Carbone listened intently, but had only one question. "Was Stanley Ferris really surprised when he stumbled over Stella's body, or could that have been an act for the benefit of anyone who happened to have a balcony seat?"

"If you're asking me if he staged the scene, the answer is no."

"You sound very certain of that, Mrs. Kennedy. Why?"

"Your suspect is a philanderer and a silly, pathetic old man, Detective, but not for a New York millisecond do I believe that Stanley Ferris possesses either the smarts or the spunk to shoot Stella, get rid of the gun, go back and party, return to the beach, and *act* shocked." Kate and Marlene had agreed that scenario was total fiction.

"And what do you base your opinions on?" His rasp turned ugly.

Kate stood. "Forty-five years of pillow talk with the smartest homicide detective in New York City. And my own well-honed awareness of people and their foibles." Where had that come from? Bold and brave, not to mention boastful. Next she'd be crediting Miss Marple. "If you don't have anything else, my friend is waiting."

Before Carbone could answer, she scurried out the door and smack into David Fry's chest.

"Excuse me, Mrs. Kennedy." Fry smiled, losing his balance but retaining his charm. "Our paths seemed to have crossed again."

Well aware that *she'd* bumped into him, Kate wanted only to escape from the police station. Muttering a quick apology, she circled around him, and continued toward the waiting room.

Fry called after her, "See you later." She felt too miserable to question why he would say that.

A few minutes later in the car, Marlene asked, "Feeling better?" She sounded so solicitous that Kate, unaccountably, felt annoyed.

"Yes. I'm fine now." And she was, or at least, her stomach had settled down. Her mind was still in turmoil.

Marlene took a right off Federal Highway. A white limo, a half-block long, stretched out in front of them, signaling their arrival at the Adams Family Mortuary. The gracious antebellum house, set back off the street, with a green lawn, magnolia trees, and a winding driveway, reminded Kate of a tiny Tara, complete with white columns and a verandah. What a way to go!

They parked behind a white hearse next to the funeral parlor and Kate, half joking, asked, "Do the pallbearers wear white, too?"

"Probably. When I attended Marty Rose's funeral, the undertaker and his entire staff wore white tuxedos. Kind of disconcerting, like the corpse was going off to a senior prom."

Kate shuddered.

The front door opened into a huge foyer, painted forest green, with glossy white moldings. A huge crystal chandelier was suspended from the high ceiling, and sconces on both walls held lighted candles — a bit much on a still sunny afternoon. A velvet and cane chair, artistically positioned near what appeared to be an authentic Hepplewhite desk, was empty.

Nary a soul in sight.

Kate assumed that the dead were laid out in viewing rooms, located behind the doors on either side of the foyer. And that their mourners had taken a dinner break. But where was Mr. Adams?

Marlene called out, "Anyone home?" Then groaned. "I can't believe I have to select the casket and what she'll wear and —"

"Have you ever read Stella's will? I mean as executrix, I'd think —"

"No. About three months ago, Wyndam Oberon, Stella's lawyer, kind of a sweet old guy, reminds me of Clarence in *It's a Wonderful Life*, came over, and Stella signed a new will. Two of the neighbors were witnesses. I was appointed as executrix, but none of us got to read it."

"Do you think she had any money? And if so, who inherited it? And who, if anyone, had she cut out? Or put in? An anxious heir might get Stanley Ferris off Detective Carbone's hook."

"Why hasn't her attorney called me? He found time to phone Adams and give him my number, didn't he? If I'm kept in the dark, how in the hell can I execute Stella's will?" Marlene sank into the dainty velvet chair. The cane frame appeared fragile, old, and expensive. Kate held her breath. It wouldn't be the first chair to collapse under her former sister-in-law's weight.

"Ladies, welcome! I'm Samuel Adams." A slight man, about fifty, with a bad comb-over, almost danced down the stairs, clapping his hands and smiling broadly. He wore a formal cutaway, the traditional jacket with tails, stripe pants, wide tie, and pearl-button vest, but instead of charcoal gray wool, his had been tailored in white polyester.

As Marlene struggled to get out of the chair, Mr. Adams grabbed hold of both her elbows and hoisted her up. Stronger than he looked.

Once on her feet, Marlene introduced Kate, then stepped into the man's space and peered into his eyes. "Okay, Mr. Adams, it's five-thirty. We have less than an hour to decide on Stella's hair, makeup, casket, service, music, flowers, burial site, and reception. I'll give the eulogy. And a bag piper, playing 'Amazing Grace' would be a nice touch. So, where do we start?"

Mr. Adams shepherded them through one of the doors that led, not to a viewing room, but a cozy parlor, complete with settees, over-stuffed armchairs, crocheted throws, and a faux fireplace. A touch of Cape Cod trans-ported to Palmetto Beach. He opened a glossy white folder, pulled a Mont Blanc from his inside breast pocket, and with great flair and fine penmanship, wrote on the top of a crisp sheet of paper, *Stella Sajak's Farewell.*

Somewhere between selecting the poem for the memorial card and pigs-in-the-blanket as the third canapé to be served at Ocean Vista's recreation hall reception, Kate said, "I have to go home and walk Ballou."

With Charlie's funeral arrangements still so fresh in her mind, why had she agreed to come here with Marlene? That terrible time of unrelenting grief, tempered only by squab-bling between his sons over the best phrase for his tombstone. The boys, no longer able to vie for their father's attention, had fought over who would have the last word. Yet somehow, that competition had warmed her heart and, ever so slightly, had eased her pain.

"Listen, Kate, I need to get this over with, and you just took Ballou out a few hours ago." Marlene's sharp tone jarred Kate. "Mr. Adams has viewing hours tonight." The funeral director nodded. "So, please . . . if you must go . . . to walk the dog, or whatever, take the car, then get right back here and pick me up."

"But —"

"No buts! We're invited for cocktails, and maybe dinner, at the most beautiful house in Palmetto Beach. I'm too old to let this golden opportunity pass me by." Her voice rose to a shrill. "And unless you agree to come with me, I won't let you drive my car home to walk your adorable dog."

Kate almost laughed. Marlene sounded like a spoiled child.

"Whose house?" she asked, knowing the answer, and also knowing that she'd never told Marlene about running — literally — into David Fry.

Mr. Adams, obviously hanging on every word, twirled his pen.

Marlene stared at the door. "David Fry's."

Kate considered, then rejected, making Marlene squirm and explain. Truth be told, she wanted to check out her prime suspect and where better than in his natural habitat?

"Give me the car keys. I'll pick you up in a half hour."

SEVEN

A black wreath, hanging on Ocean Vista's front door, greeted Kate. And at the lobby desk, Miss Mitford had changed into a black suit with a peplum, which must have dated back to the 1950s. The handful of residents milling around Aphrodite appeared appropriately funereal, too, wearing grave expressions and speaking in hushed tones.

Mary Frances Costello, dressed in a black linen sheath, stood in the center of the circle, looking very much like mourner-in-chief. A major attitude adjustment. At lunch, she'd openly expressed her dislike and jealousy of Stella.

Giving Kate a sad little smile, Mary Frances broke away from the somber group. "I just heard that Marlene is planning Stella's funeral. Can that be true?"

Recognizing an Irish instinct to, if not keen, at least be a prominent part of any wake, Kate chose her words carefully. "Yes, it's true. Stella's attorney, following his client's wishes, requested that Marlene, as executrix of the will, handle the arrangements."

Mary Frances sniffed. "I know Marlene is an old friend of yours and a former sister-in-

61

law to boot, but come on, Kate, the woman has no taste. Stella would want a quiet dignity. What she'll get is soap opera drama, with Marlene playing the Susan Lucci role."

Kate bit her lip, suppressing an urge to lash out. "I've been to at least three funerals that Marlene planned — all monuments to good taste — including my brother-in-law's." Kate saw no need to mention the white doves that Marlene had released during Kevin's burial at Calvary Cemetery, or the massive amount of poop that they'd dropped all over the neighboring graves and Father Shea's shoes. "We should respect Stella's judgment."

Kate savored the irony. She, not the ex-nun, was coming off like Mother Superior.

"It's Marlene's judgment I'm worried about. Rumor has it that she asked Stanley to sing 'Send in the Clowns' at the service."

God, could that be possible? "You'll have to excuse me, Mary Frances, I have to go."

As she waited for the elevator, Kate overheard Mary Frances tell the other mourners, "At least we can thank God that Nancy Cooper is writing the obituary."

When Kate walked in the door, Ballou gave a happy woof and jumped up to greet her. "Hey, down, down."

His sharp little claws hit her just below the knee and hurt. When she bent to pet him, he engulfed her hand in his mouth, his ultimate gesture of affection, once reserved only for Charlie. Over the past six months, Ballou and Kate had grown closer. Though she still thought of the Westie as Charlie's dog, their mutual loss had forged a bond.

"Now I have to wash my hands," she grumbled, but sensed that Ballou saw right through her. When she came back with the leash, his yips came sharp and clear.

"Hold still while I get this on!" Kate said as Ballou nipped her leg and wriggled wildly. As always, the moment the leash was in place, he turned into a model citizen, ready to go anywhere.

On the beach, Ballou trotted, importantly, ahead of Kate.

Following his lead, skirting around the yellow crime scene tape and heading south, away from the pier, Kate was chatting away, totally engaged in her one-sided conversation with Charlie. At least today, she had a fresh topic.

"I'm sure Stanley didn't kill Stella, but how can I convince that dunderhead Carbone? Oh, Charlie, you'd turn him into shredded wheat and eat him for breakfast. He scoffed at my David Fry theory and I just ran away. God, I need a plan of action. And here's what I'm thinking: Why don't I steal one of yours? Tonight, I'll open those bloody boxes, dig out your files, and study your strategies."

As if Charlie had answered her — and maybe in some sense he had — Kate rapidly made three decisions. First thing tomorrow morning, she'd call the *Sun-Sentinel* and see what, if anything, their circulation department knew about Timmy's apparent vanishing act. Next she'd check out Sea Breeze Inc.'s ice rink and resort hotel site — a hotbed of graft and payoff accusations — on Palmetto Beach's oceanfront. Why had two other Broward County towns spurned David Fry's proposal? Were he and his company guilty of those corruption charges? Stella Sajak certainly had believed they were. Then, she'd pay a visit to Nancy Cooper, who must have learned something about Stella's mysterious past while gathering material for her obituary.

Gulping the salt air and feeling almost frisky, Kate broke into a run, much to Ballou's delight.

Twenty minutes later, she tooted the horn at Marlene, who was lounging against a hearse, smoking a cigarette.

"Where have you been, Kate? We're more than fashionably late!"

"Put that cigarette out now and hop in the car, or we'll be even later."

Marlene scrambled into the passenger seat, adjusted the seat belt to accommodate her midsection, and pulled down the passenger side mirror. "What a fright! Keep the car steady, I need to fix my face."

As Kate backtracked toward the Intercoastal, Marlene whipped out a cosmetic case and reapplied her grape lipstick. Then she pointed her lip-liner pencil at Kate. "You saw David Fry in the police station, didn't you? But you never said anything. Why?"

"You're asking me why? When you never bothered to tell me that you not only saw Fry, but went ahead and accepted a cocktail and dinner date with him."

"Well, I figured you wouldn't go. I decided to wait and see if I could charm you into it — but instead, you jumped at the chance. Then you went home to change your clothes . . . and I'm all wrinkled."

"Wait a minute! I walked Ballou and got sandy . . ."

"Whatever. You're a tough one to read, Kate Kennedy. If I live to be one hundred, I'll never understand you."

"Come on, Marlene, you should have known that I'd go. David Fry could be our killer. This may be our only chance to question him."

"Don't jerk the wheel!" Marlene dipped a brush into green eyeshadow, then swept it across her right eyelid. "I'd like to do more than question him."

Kate, knowing Marlene's history with, and penchant for, rogues, changed the subject.

"Are Stella's funeral plans all set?"

"That lawyer, Oberon, called Adams from Jacksonville and I finally got to speak with him. Stella didn't want a church service and she asked to be cremated. We'll have a visitation at the funeral parlor on Friday night — I guess you can't call it a viewing with no body — and a memorial service on Saturday morning, followed by a reception at Ocean Vista. And I'll scatter her ashes over the sea."

"Will her attorney be back by Friday?"

"Yes, indeedy. I'm meeting him at Stella's apartment tomorrow morning for the reading of the will. Apparently, the cops will have finished up there."

"Reading of the will? There must be heirs, right? Maybe you're an heiress as well as an executrix!"

Marlene coated her left eyelashes with inky mascara. "Maybe!"

The setting sun behind David Fry's pale yellow mansion glimmered in the last vestige of daylight, as it seemed to sink into the water.

"Lives large, doesn't he?" Marlene sounded breathless. Kate braced herself.

Large was an understatement. The property had to be half an acre, sprawling by South Florida waterfront standards, and the yacht docked on the Intercoastal — literally, Fry's backyard — looked as if it could cross the Atlantic with ease.

Kate pulled into a driveway paved in marble and parked behind a new red Beetle. Another guest? Or did Fry own a Volkswagen as well as an SUV?

The heavy oak front doors flew open and Nancy Cooper rushed out with David Fry in hot pursuit. Fry caught up to Nancy and grabbed her briefcase rather roughly, then immediately released his grasp when he spotted Marlene's convertible.

Nancy, perhaps not noticing their car, screamed, "You'll pay for this, David!"

Kate pressed her palm on the horn and held it there — the blaring sound carried across the Intercoastal.

Nancy and David froze, as if at attention.

Marlene rolled down her window and yelled, "Hey, why don't we all go inside for cocktails and conversation?"

It was growing darker by the second. The pale moon and the lights from the yellow house cast long shadows. Neither Fry nor Cooper seemed capable of moving.

Kate took her hand off the horn and jumped out of the car.

Nancy spoke first. "David and I were having a teensy squabble over my approach to an upcoming article on the Sea Breeze's party to launch the ice rink. This silly man doesn't seem to realize that any publicity is good publicity." Having made a far quicker recovery than Fry, who remained frozen,

Nancy tapped on his forearm. "Isn't that right, David?"

"Oh . . . yes . . . right." He sounded dazed. Then a smile — forced, but firm — and his Cary Grant demeanor reemerged. Kate strained to watch his face in the growing darkness. Fascinating. Scary.

"Ladies," he said as Marlene joined them, "I'm so very sorry. This distasteful scene must have appeared so . . ." He stopped, seemingly stumped, then rushed on, "But I assure you, this was nothing more than a lapse in judgment and a burst of misplaced emotion."

Nancy grimaced. "Well, I'm off." She turned to Fry. "And don't you have a meeting in a few minutes?"

He made a big show of trying to see his Rolex. "Oh, my, yes. Sorry again, ladies. This all came up rather suddenly. I'll have to give you a rain check on those drinks."

Before either Marlene or Kate could answer, Nancy jumped into the Beetle and sped off.

Fry gave a stiff little bow, turned, and walked back to his house.

Marlene called after him, in a shout that could be heard in Boca, "Don't you worry, David Fry, I shall return."

EIGHT

It wasn't anything like the movies. Marlene, expecting a more formal gathering — after all, the reading of a will should be a somber occasion — had risen at eight o'clock, struggled into pantyhose and a too-tight black dress, and finally located her good black leather pumps under a pile of year-old dark laundry, only to be greeted by Wyndam Oberon, in a pink golf shirt. No wonder South Florida casual drove Kate crazy.

"Welcome, Ms. Friedman." He glanced at his watch. "You're early. The others haven't arrived. May I serve you coffee or tea? Mary Frances Costello has very kindly provided the refreshments." Oberon drawled out the word *refreshments* into a paragraph. "That lovely lady has gone back to her apartment for a plate of homemade cookies, but" — the attorney gestured toward the white Formica coffee table laden with fruit salad, bagels, and a divine-looking crumb cake — "please do try one of her delicious tea sandwiches."

How weird it felt, sitting in the sun-filled living room where they'd played Hearts so often, knowing that Stella Sajak would never again deal a Queen of Spades. Residual anger

69

raced through Marlene's mind, closely shadowed by guilt. Strange how Stella, a liar and a cheat, had chosen another liar and cheat to serve as her executrix.

Marlene sank into the beige chenille couch, wondering how the hell she'd get up again, and for the first time or, at least, for as long as she could remember, turned down an egg salad sandwich. Her postmortem analysis of Stella's devious ways had almost taken away Marlene's appetite. And she'd be damned if she'd eat anything that Mary Frances had made, though the sandwiches looked delicious — their cutoff crusts reflecting nun-like neatness.

Just how had Mary Frances wormed her way into the will reading, anyway? God! Could the dancing nun be one of the heirs? And who might the others be? Was Kate right? Could Marlene be an heiress? A warm, almost sexual rush flooded her loins. Greed trumped guilt. Now wouldn't that be a nice bonus in addition to the executrix fee? Did Stella have any real assets beyond the condo and a few pieces of good jewelry?

"You've served as executrix before, have you, Ms. Friedman?" Oberon sat on the edge of a navy and beige plaid armchair.

"Have I ever!" Marlene struggled into an upright position and reached for a sandwich, acknowledging that her lack of willpower would probably be the death of her, but then deciding what the hell — you have to die from something and there must be far worse causes of death than egg salad on whole wheat. Even Mary Frances's egg salad. "For my last husband. He was the only one of the three who had a will."

"Your other husbands died intestate?" Oberon sounded horrified.

"As far as I know, my first husband is still very much alive and he might have a will by now. I'd turned nineteen on the day our marriage was annulled — my twenty-two-year-old bridegroom, a rather dashing Marine, already had a wife when he'd married me. I haven't seen him since the Eisenhower administration, but according to his last Christmas card, Walter's now on his sixth wife and living in Roswell, New Mexico."

Oberon laughed. "Where else?"

Marlene devoured her tea sandwich in one bite and reached for another. "And Kevin, my second husband, and I were divorced, but we er . . . remained . . . er . . . connected."

This time the lawyer frowned.

Marlene decided her first impression had been skewed; she didn't like Oberon. Way too prissy.

"His twin brother, Charlie, was married to my best friend, Kate. So, even though Kevin and I had been divorced, we were still a family, Mr. Oberon."

"I see," Oberon said. Clearly, he didn't.

"Why, Kevin even came to my third

wedding." Marlene, enjoying herself, giggled. "Said he had to waltz with the bride."

Oberon blinked rapidly, but he appeared to be all ears.

"I didn't know it at the time, but Kevin had been diagnosed with lung cancer. That man smoked more than Humphrey Bogart and John Wayne put together. Every waking minute he'd have a Camel dangling from his lip. On the job. Driving that funny-looking little Nash. Even in bed." Marlene smiled. Especially in bed. God, despite Kevin's cancer, how she wished that she could light up right now, but there were no ashtrays in Stella's apartment. She reached for another sandwich.

"Anyway, when Kevin died, I planned his funeral. No will. No money. He'd gambled his life away. But by then, I was married to a kind man with more than enough money to give Kevin a proper sendoff. White orchids and white doves at the grave. Caviar and champagne at the wake."

Oberon's closed arms signaled disapproval, but he nodded, seeming to want to hear more.

"Jack Weiss, my third husband, was the love of my life." Marlene winked at the attorney. "So far."

"Why would you have felt responsible for your ex-husband's funeral, Ms. Friedman?"

"Because I loved him, too, Mr. Oberon."

The lawyer's lips formed a perfect O, but a sharp knock grabbed his attention. He closed his mouth and went to open the door.

Nancy Cooper, chic in a lightweight aqua wool suit, her blond hair pulled back and caught in a matching bow, entered, followed by Mary Frances, wearing a black jumpsuit — somber and sexy, no easy trick — and carrying a plate of chocolate chip cookies.

As Mary Frances placed her goodies on the table, Nancy's eyes met, then immediately looked away from, Marlene's.

"I didn't expect to see you so soon again, Nancy. How's David Fry? He certainly seemed out of sorts last evening, didn't he?" Marlene showed no mercy. "Was he afraid of you? Or was he threatening you?"

Wyndam Oberon raised a spiky white eyebrow. "What's that scoundrel Fry up to now?"

After an audible gulp, Nancy said, "No comment. As a member of the fourth estate, I claim the fifth. A journalist never reveals her source, but you can read all about Mr. Fry in tomorrow's *Palmetto Beach Gazette*."

Marlene pounced. "So he was threatening you! I knew it."

Nancy looked smug. "I must admit that I've scooped the *Sun-Sentinel*. It's such a drag that the *Gazette* only comes out once a week . . . just don't miss tomorrow's edition."

"Doesn't anyone want a cookie?" Mary

Frances passed the plate under Marlene's nose.

What's a girl to do? Marlene took two.

"Well, Miss Cooper, tomorrow I will read your scoop with relish, but right now, I have a will to read." Oberon chuckled over what he obviously considered his clever play on words. "Would you and Miss Costello please be seated?"

The lawyer snapped open his briefcase and pulled out some legal-size papers.

So they must be in the will. Marlene met Mary Frances's wide-eyed eagerness and smiled. Alive, Stella had been strident and stingy. In death, would she be gracious and giving?

Marlene certainly hoped so, but at the moment she was more intrigued with Nancy's story and how her attitude toward David Fry kept changing.

Last night Nancy had seemed frightened, trying to get away from Fry; however, she'd provided him with a bizarre cover story, that "teensy squabble" over a PR article. Then, totally out of nowhere, she'd reminded him about a "meeting," giving him an excuse to escape from Kate and Marlene's questions. Yet this morning Nancy sounded ready to crucify Fry in print. Would the true story appear in tomorrow's *Gazette*? Somehow Marlene doubted that. Why would a society reporter be assigned to cover a CEO's crooked business dealings? What the hell was really going on between Nancy Cooper and David Fry?

By the time Marlene turned her attention back to Oberon, he'd finished the preliminaries.

"And now for you lovely ladies." The attorney removed his Ben Franklin glasses, smiled, then ruffled the papers in his right hand.

Putting her suspicions on hold, Marlene focused on Wyndam Oberon.

"I want you all to know that Mrs. Sajak treasured your friendship and has remembered each of you in her will." The lawyer put his glasses back on and read, "To the members of my Hearts club, I leave the following items, carefully selected to match the recipient's personality and talents."

Marlene sighed. This should be good.

"To Mary Frances Costello, I bequeath my Llardro dancer and my mother-of-pearl rosary beads blessed by His Holiness, during my visit to Rome."

"Like I don't already have twenty-two rosaries." Mary Frances covered her mouth, as if to stop the words, but it was too late.

Wyndam Oberon, ignoring the interruption, rolled on. "To Nancy Cooper, I bequeath my considerable collection, over five hundred issues, of *Women's Wear Daily* and my signed biography of the late Elsa Maxwell."

Served Nancy right. She'd just inherited decades of outdated fashion and gossip. And judging by the puzzled look on her face, a book about a long dead society columnist that she'd never heard of.

"Finally, to Marlene Friedman Gorski Kennedy Weiss, I bequeath the mounted stag's head over my bed. It's always been an inspiration to me. And Marlene Friedman is also entitled to an executrix fee, which I trust she will refuse."

In the dead silence that followed, a key could be heard turning the lock on the condo's front door.

Marlene whipped her head around, just as the front door opened, and a good-looking man in his mid-sixties entered.

"Stella, where are you, Sweetie?"

Mary Frances jumped up and shouted, "Who are you?"

The man smiled. Smashing, Marlene thought. Lean and taut like a tiger on the prowl.

"I'm sorry. I didn't know Stella had company." The man strode across the room, his hand extended to Mary Frances. "I'm Joe Sajak. Stella's husband."

NINE

Kate, who'd spent the morning poring over Charlie's files, was getting nowhere fast with the circulation department at the *Sun-Sentinel*. The manager had gone off to a meeting, but his assistant had picked up his phone and agreed to answer Kate's questions.

"So, the truck drivers drop the papers off at selected corners all over Broward County, and then the homeless guys — they're mostly homeless — sell them." The young woman's Bronx accent sounded nasal and jaded, like Kate's cousins on her mother's side.

"Does the newspaper pay these men a salary?"

"Nah. They keep whatever they get. Gives them an incentive. The more papers they sell and the more money they make, the happier our advertising department is. And, ya know, it's the ads that keep us in business."

"Well, do you have any employment records on a man named Timmy? I'm sorry I don't have his last name. He left his post on Tuesday afternoon, and never showed up yesterday. He works the corner of A1A and Neptune Boulevard; he's been there for years. I'm worried about him."

"Well, no." The young woman chuckled. "These guys are always taking off. And they aren't real employees. It's kinda freelance work. They show up, they get the papers, they make some booze money. If they don't show up . . . there's always another bum . . . if ya get my drift."

Kate got her drift; it oozed down, blanketing Kate in depression.

She had no better luck trying to reach Nancy Cooper at the *Palmetto Beach Gazette*. The society editor's voice mail indicated that she'd be out of the office all morning. Kate left a message, saying she'd drop by around three.

After two strikes, Kate fed her frustration with a strawberry yogurt, putting banana slices and a crumbled corn muffin on top. Then she grabbed the Westie's leash. "Now settle down, Ballou. You and I are going to the pier, and by God, we're going to get to first base."

The wrecking ball, though inert at the moment, looked poised to knock down the Neptune Inn. The restaurant next to the pier, a Palmetto Beach landmark for over forty years, which served the best shrimp salad in South Florida, had been deemed expendable by Sea Breeze Inc.

Kate was standing on the southwest corner of Neptune Boulevard and A1A. Cranes and tractors and other more exotic high-tech equipment, all weapons of destruction, and all marked with Sea Breeze's logo, filled the public parking lot on the northwest side of the boulevard.

The parking lot, once enhanced, would serve the new resort hotel and ice rink, being built directly across A1A on the pier and on the beach front adjacent to it, and would charge a hefty fee. The residents of Palmetto Park, who'd used the public lot to go to the beach and to the library, located at its far end, would have to scrounge for street parking. Over a half mile of Palmetto Beach's public beach was now Sea Breeze's property. And despite the company and its CEO's unsavory reputation, this deal had been approved by the mayor and council.

Kate glanced south at Ocean Vista, a white tower, with the morning sun highlighting its art deco design. Location. Location. Location. Being right on the beach and the nearest condo to the pier always had been considered a plus — except on Friday nights when the band at the Neptune Inn had kept the left-wing condo owners awake till all hours — but now Ocean Vista's proximity had become a terrible liability.

The Sea Breeze Hotel would have three hundred rooms. No matter how much the company enlarged the public parking lot, and rumor had it that the library might be in jeopardy, there still wouldn't be enough parking places. That was why David Fry had petitioned the city council — to exercise the right of eminent domain, and buy Ocean Vista, raze it, and then, for the common good, build a parking garage.

A wave of righteous indignation swept over Kate. How dare Sea Breeze Inc. and that dreadful David Fry swoop down like vultures, and steal or swindle so much beachfront and the pier away from an inept, or even worse, crooked council, and then try to tear down her home? No wonder Stella had wanted to fight them all.

Kate segued from anger to amusement. She stared up at the blue sky as a para-sail, propelled by a motor boat, passed by. "Okay, Charlie, you win. I've just become a citizen of Palmetto Beach."

She and Ballou crossed the road and walked toward the end of the pier. Most of the stores were boarded up. The Sea Shell Shoppe had hung a sign saying FORCED OUT OF BUSINESS, next to an American flag. The yogurt kiosk, where Kate and Charlie had bought cones when they'd been down visiting Marlene, was gone — leaving only a large dark sticky stain in its wake.

Kate stared out at the ocean, its leisurely ripples lapping against the shore. Palmetto Beach boasted the widest, most beautiful expanse of sand in South Florida. A mother, with two toddlers working as apprentices, was building a sand castle. Three teenage boys — truants? — were fishing. An old couple, hand-in-hand, strolled along the water's edge. Kate ignored the pang and headed back toward the Neptune Inn.

Though still open for business, the restaurant's familiar weather-beaten brown shingles now seemed to signal defeat.

The hostess, a woman nearly as old as Kate, smiled, then petted Ballou, who nuzzled her hand. "We're serving on the patio."

"I really just want an ice tea."

"That's fine. Come, ice tea tastes better when accompanied by an ocean breeze."

Sad. This magnificent view and no customers, except for two old men, one fat, one skinny, playing Scrabble at a corner table.

As the hostess, who doubled as waitress, placed Kate's ice tea in front of her, the skinny old man spun around and removed his baseball cap. "Hey, is that you, Kate Kennedy?"

Stanley Ferris was all teeth and no hair.

The fat man sitting opposite Stanley nodded in her direction. Kate recognized him: Herb Wagner, the Neptune Inn's proprietor, at least for a few more days, and just the man Kate wanted to see.

Though becoming the prime suspect had left Stanley looking more prune-faced and wizened than ever, it hadn't made a dent in his sleaze quotient. Waving wildly, he invited

81

Kate to join him and Herb. "We can't allow a lovely lady to drink alone."

Under ordinary circumstances, she would have pled a migraine and taken a hike, but these were extraordinary times, which called for extreme measures and sacrifice. Kate picked up her glass and Ballou's leash and walked across the patio.

Herb Wagner rose and pulled out a chair for Kate.

"Hi. I'm Kate Kennedy."

"And I'm Herb Wagner, the soon-to-be-former owner of the Neptune Inn. In a few months, you'll need ice skates to navigate this space." The big man — he must have been six-six and close to three hundred pounds — had kind brown eyes and thick white hair. He reached down to ruffle Ballou's fur and received the Westie's lick of approval.

Kate nodded, smiling. "My husband and I used to come here. I'm a big fan of your shrimp salad."

"Kate's a widow." Stanley pulled his chair closer to Kate's and stuck his face under her nose. His breath smelled musty and sour. She edged her chair over, settling Ballou between her and Stanley. The Westie growled as Stanley once again attempted to move nearer to Kate, who'd turned her attention to Herb.

"I'm relatively new in town, and I just don't understand how Sea Breeze could have convinced our mayor and council to destroy your restaurant. It's all so awful."

"Do you play Scrabble, Mrs. Kennedy?"

Kate had been playing Scrabble since 1949, first with her mother, a marvelous wordsmith, crossword addict, and great teacher, then later with Charlie or Marlene. She usually beat those two by over 200 points.

"Why, yes, I do. And please call me Kate."

"So play a game with us." Herb laughed. "Stanley takes at least ten minutes before putting down a tile. I can fill you in on Sea Breeze, David Fry, and our mayor and council, while we're waiting for our turns."

"Okay." A shiver of excitement ran through Kate. She'd forgotten how competitive she was . . . how much she loved to win.

Herb had called it right. Stanley took forever to come up with a word, though, after all that deliberating, his strategy, actually, was surprisingly good.

While waiting for Stanley to play, and figuring out how to block Herb's triple-word proclivity, Kate learned the story of Sea Breeze's takeover of Palmetto Beach's prime oceanfront. Ballou fell asleep at her feet.

David Fry had arrived on the Broward County social scene about six years ago. His past, like the pasts of many South Florida newcomers, seemed vague. Some said oil money, came from Texas, didn't he? Some said a wealthy family, his courtly manners and expensively tailored tuxedos reeked of old money, came from Virginia, didn't he? No one questioned the rich bachelor's charm and social graces.

Based on Marlene's initial reaction to Fry, Kate could understand that.

By the time Fry had cut a deal with the town of Coconut Cove, selling some of his own property — for double its appraisal price — as the site for a multiplex sports arena, which Sea Breeze would erect, and then naming the mayor of Coconut Cove as vice-president of public relations for Sea Breeze, prompting a State's Attorney to launch an ongoing criminal investigation, Fry had already donated a wing to the Broward County Library and given two hundred thousand dollars to the Broward County Performing Arts Center. Most folks regarded him as an outstanding citizen.

Indeed, the Coconut Cove Chamber of Commerce had presented him with their Man of the Year Award in 2000.

The State's Attorney had slung a mess of mud, but had proved nothing.

Then, last year, David Fry had approached the Palmetto Beach City Council on the money-making advantages of having a glitzy new oceanfront resort hotel and ice skating rink replace the tired old pier and restaurant. The council, by a vote of three to one, bought into it.

Or had Fry bought them?

Herb Wagner was convinced that Brenda Walters, "a good mayor," had honestly believed that Palmetto Beach's oceanfront needed a face-lift and that Fry, a skilled con man, had swayed her vote.

"Who knows, Kate? Maybe Fry romanced her. But I'm damned sure that the two councilmen who voted for the resort complex had been bribed. Just you wait, Kate, one of those guys will wind up as Sea Breeze's next vice-president. And the other will probably be Fry's neighbor, living in a mansion on the Intercoastal."

With his story finished, Herb played his last five tiles, spelling JUICE.

Stanley got stuck with the Q.

Kate won by 210 points.

TEN

Stanley had gone to the men's room and Kate had already said good-bye to Herb and was on her way out of the Neptune Inn when she had a Columbo moment. She turned back to Herb, who was putting the Scrabble tiles into their tiny pouch, and asked, "Do you know Timmy, the *Sun-Sentinel* newsboy?" Feeling awkward about referring to Timmy as a boy, Kate stammered, "I mean man — the man who sells the papers on A1A."

"Sure do." Herb placed the pouch into the box, put the Scrabble board on top of it, then covered the box. "I stopped my home delivery decades ago. The wife and I" — he gestured toward the woman who doubled as hostess and waitress — "put in a sixteen-hour day, so I read the paper here. Timmy always brought it to the kitchen door."

"But he didn't bring it today?"

Herb faced away from the morning sun and peered at Kate. His kind brown eyes were curious. "No. Nor yesterday either. I had to go out and buy a *Herald* from the other guy. Then this morning, a new person — a woman — was selling the *Sun-Sentinel*." Kate hadn't noticed her.

"Can you remember the last time you saw Timmy?"

"Why are you asking me these questions, Kate?" Herb sounded shrewd, yet more puzzled than annoyed. "Could Timmy's disappearance have anything to do with Stella Sajak's death?"

Kate shrugged. "Maybe."

Herb nodded. "Sometime late on Tuesday afternoon. Before cocktail hour. Maybe four. Timmy stopped by for a drink."

"Was that unusual?"

"Well, he ordered a martini. Not his usual. Timmy was a ball and beer guy. Said he had something to celebrate — that he'd come into some real money and he planned on putting a down payment on a little shack out on Powerline. Not much of a house, but it sure would beat those roach-filled homeless shelters, or the beach, where he'd been sleeping."

Kate held Herb's eyes. "This is important, Herb. Did he say how he came into that money?"

"No. Actually, he sang the first line of 'There is Nothing Like a Dame,' then raised his glass. Like a toast. I went to wait on one of Fry's construction workers — probably the same guy who'll bulldoze my bar — and when I got back, Timmy was gone."

"Odd how he just vanished. Timmy was reliable, wasn't he?"

Herb nodded. "Showed up at seven-thirty every morning with my paper. Just in time for my second cup of coffee. I'd sit out here on the patio, take a breather, do the cross-word puzzle, then go in and start preparing lunch." Sadness tinged his words.

Herb Wagner's business would, literally, be destroyed . . . and with it, he'd be losing his daily routine that had spanned forty-odd years.

"I'm so sorry, Herb." Kate, knowing how painful that kind of loss could be, almost whispered the words. She wanted to reach out and touch his shoulder.

"Come on, Kate, it looks like rain." Stanley had returned from the men's room. "I'll walk you and Ballou home."

How strange that Stanley's wheeze irritated rather than concerned her. She felt more like Cinderella's cruel stepmother than Beaver's perfect Mom.

"So let's go. We'll walk; we'll talk." Stanley's wheeze had become a wheedle.

Though her mind raced like Seabiscuit, as she reached for an excuse, she came up short.

So, with a farewell to Herb, she and a reluctant Ballou followed Stanley through the door, no doubt leaving the Neptune Inn for the last time.

The slightly fishy, yet pleasant, smell of the sea mixed with the scent of pine trees and azaleas almost made Kate forget that Stanley Ferris was walking beside her.

But then his "we'll talk" became a monologue, and she became a captive audience of one.

"I could be in serious trouble, Kate. You realize that I'm Carbone's prime suspect. That man is so thick, he actually believes that I had an affair with Stella and then killed her because I'd moved on." Stanley stamped his foot, eliciting a growl from Ballou. "Something Mary Frances told him led to that conclusion, but the truth is I never slept with Stella and had no reason to want her dead."

Kate wondered why Mary Frances — who'd said that she *hadn't* told Detective Carbone about Stella and Stanley's long, intimate conversation at the Halloween party — apparently had.

The nuns of Kate's childhood had been nothing if not consistent. Mary Frances's only constant seemed to be caprice.

Out of nowhere Kate's Town Hall senior moment flickered, then faded. Why couldn't she remember? Stanley had been there, one arm draped over Stella and the other draped over Marlene, when Stella had agreed to meet with the mayor. And of course, David Fry had overheard that date being arranged.

"Stanley, can you remember what, exactly, Stella said at the Town Hall, just before the

89

mayor agreed to meet with her the following morning?"

He glanced at Kate, then winked. "Not really. Being surrounded by all you beautiful women must have distracted me."

Good Lord! The revolting little man was actually flirting with her. Kate hoped her disgust didn't show.

"And of course, Mary Frances had spotted me with my arms around Stella and Marlene. I could tell she wasn't happy."

So, Mary Frances had been there, observing. Observing what? Kate cursed the almost-memory that refused to emerge from her senior moment.

Stanley, wheezing worse than ever — why didn't the man see a doctor? — picked up where he'd left off. "And the vicious rumor that I killed Stella in order to become president of Ocean Vista is defamation of character."

Kate laughed. She hadn't meant to, but there it was, a robust guffaw, right in Stanley's face.

"What's so damn funny, Kate? I might be arrested any minute. God, the police are getting a search warrant. They'll turn my apartment upside down."

Kate, seizing the opportunity, spoke. "Well, that should clear you. They won't find anything, will they?"

Stanley blushed, the red color, rising on his

wizened, mean little face, highlighting puppet lines and a turkey neck. He stared down, as if searching for something on the sidewalk.

Ballou tugged on his leash, seeming to urge Kate to move along and let Stanley stew.

All traces of June Cleaver thrown to the wind, Kate asked again, "The police won't find anything, right?"

Stanley kept his eyes to the ground. "Well, there are some favorite sites on my computer that might — er — put me in a bad light. And you know, there are ways for the police to tell how often a person visits a Web site."

Porn? Kiddie porn? Had Charlie sent her that message? Or had she thought of it herself? Either way, Kate sensed something sordid, and wished that Ballou would take a bite out of Stanley's skinny ankle.

They approached Ocean Vista's flower-lined driveway in uncomfortable silence. A red Beetle, illegally parked, blocked the right side of the driveway.

Nancy Cooper bounded out of the condo.

Kate called out to her. "I left a message on your office answering machine. I'm going to stop by this afternoon around three."

Stanley wheezed. "I'm going around back. See you ladies later."

Nancy, looking very smart but appearing flustered, said, "I doubt I'll have any time today, Mrs. Kennedy."

"It's about David Fry and Sea Breeze.

You'll want to hear this."

Nancy's expression changed. Not warm, but certainly more receptive. "I'm on deadline today, but I guess I can spare you a few minutes. I'm meeting with a source at two, but I should be back in the office by three."

Nancy Cooper brushed past Kate, jumped into the red Beetle, and drove off.

God Almighty, Kate thought, that woman believes she's Bob Woodward.

In the lobby, Marlene was tête-à-tête with Mary Frances, whispering like teenagers in front of Aphrodite's statue. Both women wore black outfits and dazed expressions.

Kate knew that Marlene had gone to the reading of Stella's will this morning. Did Mary Frances's black jumpsuit indicate that she'd been there, too?

Ballou, delighted to see Marlene, led a more than intrigued Kate over to her, just as a slim gray-haired man came out of the elevator and approached them from the other side.

"Kate!" Marlene, looking from the man to Kate, spoke with impish delight. "I'd like you to meet Stella's husband, Joe Sajak. Turns out he isn't dead after all. We're just heading into the dining room for lunch. Why don't you just take Ballou upstairs, and then join us?" She bent to allow Ballou to lick her hand.

ELEVEN

Accompanied by a blast of thunder and sheet lightning that flashed over the sea, the rains came. As Kate entered Ocean Vista's dining room, drops the size of lollipops sloshed its windows. Outside on the beach, sunbathers and swimmers frantically closed umbrellas, swooped up towels and totes, and scurried to shelter. After six months, she remained amazed by the capricious South Florida weather. Blue skies and sunshine could morph into dark clouds and teeming rain in a matter of minutes.

Marlene, Mary Frances, and Joe sat at a window table, their heads turned toward the beach, watching the storm, a definite attention grabber. The waves were rising high, then crashing against the shore, and the surfers, who always showed up so quickly that they appeared to be on call, were riding their crests.

Kate, just inside the door, waited and watched.

Jolted by the appearance of a *supposedly* long dead husband, just in time for his wife's funeral — and how Agatha Christie was that? — Kate had rapidly reviewed her theories

93

about Stella's murder while riding up and down in the elevator. Throwing Joe Sajak into the mix, Kate came up with more questions than answers. The two most nagging: When had he arrived in South Florida? And did this mystery man have a motive?

Charlie had believed that you can tell as much about a suspect by his body language as you can by his responses to an interrogation, so she observed the cozy trio.

There was an empty chair between Marlene and Mary Frances, who had book-ended Joe Sajak. As the storm raged, Mary Frances placed a less than tentative hand on Joe's arm. More clutching than comforting. Marlene, in total violation of the dining room's policy, lit a Marlboro and blew a smoke ring, which hovered over Joe's head. The man in the middle appeared nervous, first patting Mary Frances's hand, then jerking up his arm to wave away the smoke ring, forcing her to release her grip. Marlene, after whispering something in Joe's ear that elicited a nod, put out her cigarette in a coffee cup. Wait till Tiffani saw that.

A cacophony of thunder made Kate's heart jump. A lifetime ago, to quell her fear, Kate's mother had assured her that thunder was the sound of angels bowling. If so, Gabriel — or maybe Charlie — must have thrown a strike. Kate smiled, squared her shoulders, and crossed the room.

She hoped that Ballou, home alone, wasn't too frightened.

For the second time in a matter of hours, a man jumped up and pulled out a chair for her. It felt strange. Almost eerie. At the condo closing, Charlie had pulled out Kate's chair, sat down himself, winked at her, and using the Mont Blanc that she'd given him last Christmas, proudly signed the ownership papers, then dropped dead. From that day to this day, she'd been pulling out her own chairs.

Seated between Marlene and Mary Frances, Kate leaned across the latter to thank Joe Sajak. His smile dazzled; some dentist had made a small fortune capping those teeth. So many senior men seemed to be spending big bucks and ending up with far whiter teeth in their old age than they ever had in their youth.

"I never saw that shirt before. Silk, isn't it?" Marlene sounded surprised. Or peeved? Kate couldn't decide.

In an impish moment, counting on winding up between two women wearing black, Kate had changed, putting on a bright melon shirt, soft and silky, that she'd bought — but never worn — just before she and Charlie had moved to Palmetto Beach.

Giving Marlene a quick nod, confirming that the shirt was silk, Kate turned to Mary Frances. "You all must have had an interesting morning."

"Well, I'd say so." Mary Frances laughed. Nervous, not happy laughter. "Like that old movie where Irene Dunne shows up after Cary Grant has believed that she'd been dead for seven years and was about to marry. Gail Patrick, I think. Anyway Irene, not being dead, turns everyone's life upside down."

Kate remembered the movie — *My Favorite Wife* — recalling its old-fashion charm, and then decided that, despite what Marlene thought, David Fry was no Cary Grant.

"Except Stella always knew that I wasn't dead." Joe Sajak spoke in a deep baritone. Almost too deep and too booming for such a narrow, compact man. "And I never suspected that Stella was dead." He shook his head, coming across as sad and rueful. Kate didn't buy it. Why wasn't he more grief-stricken? Or even just more surprised? Or making phone calls to friends? Or heading over to the funeral parlor? "I truly loved that gal, though I readily admit that we had a most unusual marriage."

"Joe was just about to explain — um — his and Stella's arrangement when the storm began," Marlene said, letting Kate know that while she might have missed Act One — the reading of the will and Joe's entrance — Act Two hadn't really started yet. "Why don't we order? Then, while we're eating lunch, Joe can tell all."

Marlene, as usual, had her priorities.

96

As Tiffani arrived with the menus, Kate wondered if Detective Carbone had any idea that Joe Sajak was alive and well and ordering lunch in Ocean Vista's dining room?

Over salmon and salad, Joe Sajak talked. "I've known Stella most of my life. We married young, over forty-five years ago, but we haven't really lived together as man and wife for a long time. Since we never had any kids, when Stella wanted to move to Florida and I didn't, we decided to go our separate ways, but we never divorced. Never even talked about it. We'd agreed at the time that if one of us ever fell in love and wanted to marry someone else, we'd reevaluate our situation. But neither of us ever brought that subject up again. Stella would come up North once or twice a year. We'd go off to Europe or the Grand Canyon or take a cruise together. Then we'd each go back to our own lives." He paused and tasted a tomato.

A drum roll of thunder careened through the dining room.

"You never came down here?" Mary Frances spoke Kate's thought.

"No. Never." Joe shook his head. "And that, too, had been Stella's call. She said she needed 'her own identity — her own life' and I respected that. An odd relationship, I know, but it worked for us."

"Well," Marlene said, "was Mr. Oberon aware that you existed?"

"Certainly. As her husband, I was Stella's heir."

"Really?" Marlene frowned.

"Oh, I know there were other bequests, but I receive the bulk of the estate. Oberon had been trying to contact me to tell me about Stella's death and the reading of the will, but I was on my way here, then off sailing." Joe Sajak smiled, then continued in that too-deep baritone, "I had a quick word with Wyndam before I left the apartment. He's going to call the police and let them know that I've finally arrived. I'm sure they'll want to talk to me."

The crescendo in Kate's mind competed with the thunder. So Detective Carbone had known that Joe Sajak wasn't dead. And Sajak, as heir apparent, had a motive. And since he'd never visited Florida before, why now?

"I'll just bet the police want to talk to you," Mary Frances said.

A sudden silence descended over the table and in the heavens. As Tiffani approached to clear away their dishes, Kate could hear her charm bracelet clang.

Then another burst of thunder rocked the room. Kate watched through the window as the wind whipped the sand and sent it flying, and the palm trees' leaves swayed like hula dancers. She hoped Ballou wouldn't be too frightened.

Could a hurricane be blowing up out there? Kate doubted it. South Florida anchorpersons and weatherpersons tracked any hint of an impending hurricane, savoring its name and exploring its devastation potential, minute by minute, for days on end, before the storm hit — or more likely, missed.

Over dessert, Marlene reviewed Stella's funeral plans, starting with Friday night's wake, moving on to the service on Saturday morning, followed by the reception in the recreation room and, finally, the scattering of Stella's ashes over the sea.

A tear formed in Joe Sajak's eye, and dropped onto his sundae, which he then shoved away.

"That sounds right. Stella always loved the sea." Several more tears rolled down Joe's cheek. Mary Frances reached into her pocket and handed him a perfectly pressed, sparkling white handkerchief.

"I'd like to see Stella. Where is she? At the funeral parlor?"

"She will be. Sometime this afternoon, I think." Marlene sounded as frazzled as she looked. Her sienna tan had gone gray and her blood red lipstick had seeped into the creases around her mouth. "They're releasing the body today."

Kate pushed her rainbow sherbet to one side, suddenly consumed with Stella's cremation.

"I'd like to meet with the funeral director to review the costs." Joe wiped his eyes with Mary Frances's handkerchief, then carefully folded it and placed it next to the napkin.

Did his gesture signal no more tears?

"Of course, I'm sure you've done an excellent job as executrix, Marlene, but we all know these funeral directors can be thieves. And as the widower, I'll be the one footing the bill, now, won't I?"

Marlene opened, then shut, her mouth.

Out of the corner of her right eye, Kate saw Detective Carbone enter the room, fill it with his presence, then take three long strides in their direction.

A flash of lightning missed their window by inches, the sky turned black, thunder, loud as if Lucifer himself were bowling, deafened, and the lights went out.

At that very moment, feeling a fury that more than matched the raging storm, Kate demanded, "When, exactly, did you arrive in Palmetto Beach, Mr. Sajak?"

And Detective Carbone, who'd reached the table, said, "Yes, Mr. Sajak. I'm curious about the answer to Mrs. Kennedy's question, too."

TWELVE

They hadn't heard Joe Sajak's response because, before he could even open his mouth, Detective Carbone had *invited* him down to the police station to take his statement.

To get away from the dining room, abuzz with chatter and filled with curious stares, Kate had invited Mary Frances and Marlene to her apartment. She, too, was dying with curiosity and felt certain that those two would have some answers.

Sitting in Kate's living room, holding Ballou in her lap, Marlene said, "Is Sajak a snake? He seemed so sweet at first blush."

Wanting to say, And don't they all, Marlene? — instead Kate nodded and waited for her former sister-in-law to continue.

"I know. I know!" Marlene said. "You don't think I'd recognize a snake if it slithered up my arm!"

Kate smiled. "Well . . ."

Mary Frances, who'd been pacing, stopped and pointed a finger at Marlene. "Did you believe that cock-and-bull story that Joe Sajak told that nice Mr. Oberon?"

Kate pounced. "Did Joe Sajak say where

he'd been before he showed up at Stella's this morning?"

"Since you have such a low opinion of my judgment in men, Kate, why are you asking me about Joe's whereabouts?" Marlene raised her voice. "Aren't you afraid that my propensity for snakes will color my reportage?"

"Kate asked me, Marlene, not you, so why don't you just keep quiet for once?" Mary Frances stopped pacing and perched on the edge of the off-white couch. Kate wondered how many condos in Ocean Vista had off-white couches, probably two out of three.

The storm ended as abruptly as it had begun. Sunlight streamed through the glass doors that led to the patio, and though the plastic furniture still glistened with raindrops, all would be dry in a matter of minutes.

"Speaking of reportage" — Kate looked at Marlene — "I have an appointment with Nancy Cooper at three, so whoever wants to tell me about Joe Sajak had better talk fast."

"Nancy seems to have the goods on David Fry," Marlene said. "Though all smug hints and no hard facts — if you can believe anything that woman says — her story in tomorrow's *Gazette* should expose him."

"Good," Kate said, "maybe she'll give me a preview."

"I wouldn't count on it." Mary Frances shrugged. "Why don't you start the Sajak saga, Marlene? As a former teacher, I have

102

an ear for details. I'll fill in what you leave out."

Giving Mary Frances a dirty look, Marlene said, "Well, when the undead husband walked through the door — he had a key — we were already in a state of shock. You wouldn't believe the weird stuff that Stella bequeathed to me, Nancy, and Mary Frances."

"Nancy Cooper was in Stella's will?" Kate asked.

"Yes," Marlene said, putting Ballou down. "The three surviving members of the lonely Hearts club are now heiresses. Unfortunately, all we inherited was Stella's flotsam and jetsam."

Kate glanced at her watch.

"Okay, here's the abridged version." Marlene went into speed mode. "Joe Sajak arrived in Fort Lauderdale late Tuesday afternoon."

Kate's heart jumped. "Just in time to kill Stella."

"You betcha!" Marlene fumbled in her tote bag and pulled out a Milky Way. They hadn't had dessert, and since they'd been kids, Marlene never considered a meal complete without a sweet. "Sajak told Oberon he'd borrowed a boat from an old friend who kept it berthed at the Pier 66 Marina."

Kate said. "Travis McGee, I presume?"

"Travis would be too smart to lend Joe

103

Sajak his boat." Marlene laughed. "Anyway, Joe claims that he flew into Fort Lauderdale, went straight to the store, loaded up on groceries, then boarded the boat, and took off Tuesday night round eight. That, of course, would be well before Stella had been shot."

"Where did he sail to?" Kate asked.

"Said he headed north on the Intercoastal and anchored in Boynton Beach around midnight, then spent the night on board. On Wednesday morning, he sailed out of Deerfield Beach Harbor and did some fishing in the ocean. He sailed back to Pier 66 this morning and — finally — showed up at Stella's. Being away from his home in Michigan, and not having a cell phone, he never picked up Oberon's many messages and never knew that Stella had been murdered."

"But his own story doesn't give Sajak an alibi," Mary Frances said. "I mean no one else was on board. He sailed alone."

Kate nodded. "So . . . if he left Pier 66, and docked somewhere close by here, he could have hopped off the boat and arrived on the beach in plenty of time to kill Stella."

"And if, as Joe Sajak claims, he came to Fort Lauderdale to surprise Stella, why did he sail away without seeing her first?" Marlene pulled out two more Milky Ways. "Anyone want to join me?"

"To create an alibi."

Kate shook her head, both to Marlene's

Milky Way offer and May Frances's comment. "But as you just pointed out, Mary Frances, not much of an alibi."

"I don't think he's too bright. What kind of man spends all those decades in a *Same Time, Next Year* marriage?" Mary Frances twisted a red curl around her index finger, then turned and stared out the window. Could she be thinking about all those decades that she'd spent in the convent?

Having no takers, Marlene bit into another Milky Way. "The card table wasn't the only place where Stella cheated. I'll bet lots of people wanted that woman dead. God knows what devilment she'd been up to before she moved down here."

"God," Kate said, "and possibly, her widower. Marlene, when Joe Sajak returns from the police station, why don't you invite him over for dinner?"

"I'll bring dessert," Mary Frances said.

Driving over, Kate rehearsed her opening line. "So, Nancy, do you think David Fry killed Stella Sajak?"

Though the sun was shining, a burst of thunder answered her.

"Okay, Charlie, I hear you. I'll be more subtle."

The *Palmetto Beach Gazette* was located on Federal Highway, a block away from the police station and Town Hall. The three-story pink stucco Spanish-style building had pretensions toward Boca Raton's downtown flair, but fell far short. Kate pulled into the parking lot and grabbed her umbrella; it was raining again. Her Ocean Vista neighbors always said, in South Florida, if you don't like the weather, wait five minutes. Walking around to the front door, Kate hoped that today they were right.

With wet chinos and soggy shoes, she went through the oak doors, into the lobby. The air-conditioning hit her damp shirt with a cold blast. Somewhere in the rear of the building, the presses were rolling. Shivering, she checked the names list next to the elevator. Nancy Cooper's office was on the second floor. As Kate reached to press the button, the elevator door opened and David Fry stepped back to allow an attractive blonde to exit before him. Well, well, Mayor What's Her Name?

"Good afternoon, Mrs. Kennedy." Fry oozed that canned charm. "I believe you've met our mayor, Brenda Walters?"

The mayor smiled and extended her hand. "Nice to see you again, Mrs. Kennedy. I'm so sorry about your friend's death. Such a civic-minded woman. What a great loss for our town. I want you to know that the police are working round the clock to find Stella Sajak's killer."

Kate felt startled. Should she be receiving

condolences on Stella's death? She'd never considered her a friend, only a neighbor, and rather a pain in the butt at best, but she said, "Thank you."

The mayor smiled, showing lots of white teeth and not unattractive crinkles around jade green eyes. "Wyn has invited me to the memorial. I'll see you there." So Stella's — and the condo's — nemesis would be at the Ocean Vista memorial. Talk about the enemy at the gate.

David Fry, looking solemn, said, "I'll be at the service, too." He took Brenda Walters's arm. "I'm sorry to dash off, but we're running late." His smile dazzled, too. Fry, the mayor, and Joe Sajak must have shared the same dental plan. "Good day, Mrs. Kennedy. I'll be seeing you."

How could such obsequious politeness sound so ominous?

Kate crossed in front of him, stepped into the elevator, and pushed 2. As the door was closing, she said, "You can count on that, Mr. Fry."

So Fry was cozy with the mayor and the mayor was cozy with Wyn Oberon, and dollars to doughnuts, Fry and Walters had just visited Nancy Cooper. What a tangled web of a town.

A plump older woman — probably older than Kate, who recently had been noticing how many elderly women were still working

— sat at the desk in the *Gazette*'s reception area. Its white stucco walls were cluttered with laminated newspaper headlines and pictures in black frames.

"Take a load off your feet, sweetie," the woman told Kate, pointing to a faux leather black couch. Kate sighed. South Florida's decor, like South Florida's population, seemed filled with fakes. "Her majesty is holding court, but the Knave of Hearts should be out in a minute."

Kate, suddenly feeling very tired, sank into the couch. It smelled like plastic, reminding her of the pink, ruffle-trimmed plastic cushions on her mother's kitchen chairs. She could see her mother, wearing a crisply ironed apron, sitting at the table, with its pink, flowery, linoleum-backed tablecloth, pasting saving stamps into a booklet. When the stamps added up to $18.25, she'd buy a War Bond — and put Kate's name on it. "One day, these bonds will mature and send you to Marymount, Kate." But by the time Kate had been ready for college, her mother had died, and they sold the bonds to bury her, and even with a scholarship, Kate's father could scrape up enough for only two years at Hunter, then Kate had gone to work for Eastern Airlines.

Funny how a smell or a touch or a taste could transport you back to the 1940s. Maybe would-be time travelers should concentrate more on the five senses.

She heard a door open — nothing wrong with her hearing, but she had trouble believing her eyes. Stanley Ferris came strutting back into the reception room, wearing a white linen sports jacket and a black silk shirt.

"Yo, Kate, if you're here to see Nancy Cooper, let me warn you — though she's only second vice-president, she has stepped into Stella's role as condo crusader and is even meaner than the original."

When Kate said nothing, he continued, "Listen, do you like to dance? I'm going to Ireland's Inn tonight and I can really cut a rug. I bet you still have a few good moves left."

Stanley had discovered Stella's body on the beach on Tuesday night and by Thursday afternoon he felt ready to jitterbug. Kate wanted to scream.

Nancy Cooper pushed open the door that Stanley had just closed. "Kate Kennedy, come on in! But make it snappy. I'm on deadline."

THIRTEEN

Unlike the very well put together Ms. Cooper, her office looked worse than Marlene's apartment. Empty coffee cups, wads of crumpled-up tissues, overstuffed file folders, and sloppy piles of paper covered her desk top and spilled over onto the tiled floor. Old *Gazette*s, *Sun-Sentinel*s, and *Miami Herald*s filled much of the remaining floor space, and navigating through the sea of paper proved difficult. Even the computer looked grimy.

"Please have a seat." Nancy Cooper gestured to one of two armchairs in front of her desk. "Is it okay if I call you Kate?" Asked with the smug deference of one a generation younger.

Kate thought, why not? If you want a person to reveal secrets, you'd better be on a first-name basis. She smiled broadly, warmly. June Cleaver herself couldn't have been more motherly. "I'd like that, Nancy."

"Since I'm really pressed for time, Kate, why don't you sit down and tell me everything you know about David Fry?"

"Well, first I have a question for you." Kate rolled her eyes upward and made a silent apology to Charlie. "Do you think David Fry killed Stella Sajak?"

Nancy's eyes narrowed. "Playing Miss Marple can be a dangerous game."

No threatening tone, just a brisk, cold warning from a busy woman, who definitely knew something. But what? Kate's question hadn't seemed to surprise Nancy. Whose side was she on? David Fry's? Or as Marlene surmised, ready to expose him and his company? Or could it be something else? Something more sinister? Kate realized that she had precious little information to barter, and that Nancy must have damaging evidence about Fry — either connected to Sea Breeze's corrupt operation or to Stella's murder. Or to both. Kate sat straight and silent and waited.

After twelve seconds — Kate had counted — Nancy spoke. "Look, I'm the reporter and I'm used to gathering information, not leaking it. If you have something to tell me, please go ahead, but if not, I have three stories on deadline, with only the obit ready to roll. I still have to put the finishing touches on the other two, then I'll have to fight like the devil to get one, or maybe both, in print, so I haven't time for innuendo."

God, she really *does* think she's Bob Woodward.

"Three stories?" Kate tried to sound awed. "My, you are a busy woman. Let's see. The first is Stella's obit. Then there's the story about David Fry that you mentioned to Marlene and Mary Frances." Kate figured two sources were better than one. "And from what they said, I gather that article will expose Sea Breeze Inc. and its CEO, and maybe even Palmetto Beach's mayor and council. I ran into Fry and the mayor in the lobby and I figured you'd been interviewing them, looking for a quote or a denial. But what I'm really curious about is your third story."

Nancy started, then her eyes darted to the slim folder on the top of the pile directly in front of her.

Kate focused on the folder, too. Printed in bold black letters on its cover was: **STELLA SAJAK'S PAPERS**. Why would that file make Nancy nervous? After all, she'd probably used those papers to write the obit.

Had something in that folder given Nancy a clue to Stella's murderer? Maybe something incriminating about Joe Sajak?

"Did you know that Joe Sajak was alive?"

Nancy looked up from the folder and gave Kate a Cheshire cat grin. "No, I sure didn't, but when my story runs tomorrow, that will be *so* yesterday's news."

"Which story?" Kate ached with frustration. "The second or the third?"

Nancy stood. "Read tomorrow's edition of the *Palmetto Beach Gazette*. Now I have to end this chat."

"But . . ."

With grace and agility, obviously based on

long practice, Nancy strode around the mess on the floor and opened the door. "One piece of advice, Kate. If you know what's good for you, stay the hell away from David Fry."

When Kate arrived at the condo, the phone was ringing and Ballou was barking. Grabbing the phone, she said, "Hush."

"Well, hush to you, too, Mom." Kevin chuckled.

"Oh, Kevin, sorry, darling, I guess I'm doing too many things at once."

"That's great. You sound — I don't know — happier?"

Kate heard the hesitation in his voice.

"Yes. Happier may not be quite the right word, but certainly, I've been busy these last couple of days." Kate saw no reason to mention that she and Marlene were investigating a murder. "Getting out more."

"I'm glad. Playing bingo?"

"Ye gods, Kevin, no. But I may join a Hearts group. One of the members — er — died suddenly."

"Listen, Mom, I need to talk to you about Thanksgiving."

"Yes, will you all come down here or should —"

"Mom, Jennifer wants to take the girls skiing in Vail. Lauren could fly in from Boston and Katharine, Jennifer and I would meet her there." He paused, then coughed. "Oh . . ."

"Of course, you're more than welcome to join us. We're renting a chateau. Jen's bonus will pay for it. We'd love to have you."

"Kevin, the last time I went skiing was long before you and Peter were born. I tried the small slope, even took lessons, but failed miserably and spent most of my time as a ski bunny, sitting at the bar in the lodge, waiting for your father to get off the slopes." Her stomach gurgled. "I don't think this old rabbit would be comfortable doing that now. But you guys go. It sounds like a great family vacation."

"You really don't mind, Mom? I mean, we've always been together for Thanksgiving."

"Marlene and I will be fine. You know how much she enjoys fussing over holiday dinners. Maybe we'll start a new tradition — Thanksgiving turkey al fresco on the beach."

"And we'll all be together for Christmas at Peter's, right?"

"Yes, darling." Kate swallowed her resentment. "That's right."

When Kate hung up, she felt sad, abandoned, and foolish. A mix of emotions that further aggravated her stomach.

Jennifer Lowell Kennedy, Kevin's beautiful and brilliant wife, managed to get her own way, via charm, wile, and on occasion,

114

whining. Kate loved her, if not like a daughter, like a favorite niece. Kevin, the firefighter, worshipped his stockbroker wife, whose high-six-figure income made it possible for them to live in a brick Tudor and send Lauren, who'd inherited both her mother's brains and those fabulous Lowell cheekbones, to Harvard. Their younger daughter, Katharine, who had neither her mother's beautiful body nor her beautiful mind, was Kate's namesake and her favorite. Katharine's red hair and freckled face, with its pug nose and impish grin, not to mention her raucous, "yes I can" personality, readily identified her as Charlie's granddaughter. Well, she wouldn't be seeing either of the girls till Christmas.

Needing comfort and a cup of tea, Kate dialed Marlene.

By five, her gripe session long over, Kate was walking the beach with Marlene and talking about murder. Ballou had pranced ahead of them, doing his own investigation of a dead crab, which he now kicked some sand over.

As the still warm surf washed over her bare feet, Kate said, "Nancy Cooper may be a whistle blower, but I'm not sure whose tea kettle is boiling over. David Fry may be romancing the mayor as well as bribing the councilmen. And Nancy must have something on Stanley Ferris. I don't believe his visit to the *Gazette* today was about condo politics."

"Well, I guess we'll know tomorrow morning when we read the *Gazette*. You have no clue about the third story?"

"Only a hunch." Kate sighed. "When I asked about it, Nancy's eyes went right straight to Stella Sajak's folder. Could there be something in that folder that might lead to Stella's killer?"

"Stella gave Nancy that obit stuff months ago — in June, I think. Stella couldn't have had any idea back then that she'd be murdered on Halloween. So how could she have planted evidence? That doesn't make any sense, Kate."

"No, it doesn't . . . but . . . what if Stella left a letter or something in the folder by mistake? And what if that letter — or piece of paper — or whatever — has somehow revealed the killer's identity?"

"What do you mean? Like what kind of paper?" Marlene, raising her voice, yanked Ballou's leash, and he responded with a yelp.

"Hey, watch it, Marlene, you startled Ballou," Kate said, thinking that she'd startled Marlene. But that was crazy. Why would Marlene be concerned about what might or might not be among Stella's papers?

"I'm just thinking out loud. Nancy kept staring at that folder. I don't know, maybe I'm all wet."

A large wave crashed at their feet,

splashing them up to their knees. Their shared laughter seemed to dissipate Marlene's tension, but not Kate's curiosity. Puzzled by Marlene's reaction, frustrated by her visit to Nancy, and most of all suspicious of Joe Sajak, Kate decided to temporarily shelve the third story and move on to the widower.

"So is Joe Sajak coming to dinner?"

"I invited him about an hour ago and he accepted with 'great pleasure.' Mary Frances had spotted him in the lobby, so we knew he was out of Carbone's clutches."

"He didn't spend much time at the station, did he? I guess the good detective had no hard evidence."

"No, it must have been a quickie. Joe had been back for a while, and I wasn't his first visitor. Three widows had dropped by with casseroles before I arrived."

Kate laughed. "I guess we should be flattered that he's dining with us. What time is dinner?"

"Seven-thirty. And I've got to go. The steaks are marinating and my pound cake is cooling. And I still have to melt the fudge for my million-dollar secret frosting."

Kate decided to take two Pepcid ACs as appetizers.

FOURTEEN

Kate watched in amazement as Marlene's apartment morphed from chaos to cozy. The hostess, dressed in a gold caftan, swept the mess, ranging from unwashed undies to unpaid bills, into the closets, then drew the drapes, dimmed the lights, and filled the living room with fresh flowers and candles. Big bunches of multicolored flowers, spilling over in charming disarray from fat, round crystal bowls. Dozens of candles — in every size and shape.

"Candlelight not only makes us old broads look better, Kate, it hides the dust. I swear if Consuela doesn't come back from Cuba soon, I may have to move."

Kate wondered when and if the closets would be cleaned. Even Consuela, Marlene's long-suffering housekeeper, could do only so much. Soon the litter would take over, like the pods in *Invasion of the Body Snatchers*. Then Marlene might move; it wouldn't be the first time she'd have run away from a mess.

But for now, with the candles flickering, Sinatra singing softly in the background, the table set with Marlene's finest china, and wonderful smells coming from the kitchen, the guests would feel tranquil, anticipating a delightful dinner, never knowing that things are not always what they seem.

"How can I help?" Kate caught a glimpse of herself in the Victorian mirror hanging over the couch. Charlie would have approved. She'd dressed in her blue linen slacks and smartly cut matching top, added pearls, applied fire engine red lipstick, and remembered to put on mascara and line her eyes. Of course, in a room this dark and a mirror this dusty, anyone would find her image flattering.

"Pick up the clutter on the balcony — I've never had a visitor who didn't ask to see the ocean — and shove everything under the bed in the guest room. You'll have to rearrange a few things." Marlene's balcony, so low to the ground that it felt more like a terrace, had enough clutter to fill a thrift shop. If she'd only part with some of this junk, she could make a fortune on eBay.

Kate was sprawled on the guest room's off-white Berber carpet, trying to encircle a box under the bed, containing a Macy's mannequin — and why had Marlene saved that? — with a hula hoop, when she heard laughter coming from down the hall. Then Joe Sajak's voice, saying, "Well, you certainly look lovely tonight, Mary Frances."

The hell with this. Kate scrambled to her feet, laid the hula hoop on top of the spread, lowered the dust ruffle to conceal the junk, and smoothed her slacks. Let the games begin.

Marlene was taking drinks orders and Joe sprang to his feet as Kate entered the living room.

Mary Frances did, indeed, look lovely in a coral silk wrap dress and matching sandals.

"Hello, Kate." Joe's deep baritone was accompanied by a sad little smile. Kate wondered if he'd practiced it in front of a mirror. "I was just saying how kind you ladies are, helping a lonely old man get though this tragedy. I still can't believe Stella's gone."

Kate swept across the room and sat on the couch, planting herself between Mary Frances and her quarry. "Joe," she said, all warm and toasty, locking her eyes on his, "at a time like this, it helps to talk. Tell us about you and Stella. I'll bet she was a delightful young woman."

"More like a pugnacious little brat. We were in first grade together — I told you that — and she organized a minirevolt, protesting against the small boxes of Crayolas, demanding the larger size, that held forty-eight different colors. Our teacher, Miss Jenkins, didn't stand a chance. In less than a week she caved and every kid in the class had the bigger box of crayons." He paused and accepted a glass of white wine from Marlene. "Stella was a skinny kid, with wild black curls, great big charcoal gray eyes, and the rosiest cheeks I'd ever seen." He laughed. "I can thank her for changing my life and coloring my conversation. Anyway, that little brat sure caught my attention and I've loved her since the day I met her." He took a sip of his wine.

Kate certainly hadn't expected such a seemingly sincere and passionate response. She'd rehearsed several questions with Charlie while getting dressed, but now, completely thrown, she couldn't remember any of them.

"So you two dated all through high school?" Mary Frances placed a hand on Joe's arm and, though Kate couldn't be sure, seemed to give it a squeeze.

He turned away from Kate to answer Mary Frances.

"Well, I carried her books, passed out her protest pamphlets, and rode her back and forth on my bike all through grade school, but in our junior year, she ran for president of the student council and started dating the far more dashing captain of the football team. About broke my heart. But he dumped her for a cute blond trick — I forget her name — and Stella and I got back together."

"And when did you get married?" Mary Frances had tilted her head forward, so that her lips were inches from Joe's, and no doubt about it, she was squeezing his arm.

121

"Right after high school, I joined the Marines. Stella's mother had died by then, and her father, well, he drank too much — so we got married and moved to North Carolina."

Kate started, remembering what Marlene had said at the pool on Wednesday morning. "So when did Stella attend Northwestern?"

Joe spun around to face Kate. "Never. Why do you ask? When I was stationed in California, Stella took a few acting classes at UCLA, then enrolled in a secretarial school. Got herself a damn good job at a movie studio. She'd always wanted to be a movie star. I guess working as a stenographer at MGM was the next best thing."

Somehow Kate doubted that Stella would have agreed with Joe's conclusion.

Marlene placed a small tray of cheese and crackers on the coffee table. "Why don't you try the Brie, Joe?" She spread some on a cracker and handed it to him. "You know, I spent a lot of time with Stella. On the beach. Playing Hearts. At condo meetings. She never mentioned living in California, but she certainly mentioned graduating from Northwestern — even wanted that *fact* to be included in her obituary."

Reaching for the cracker, Joe said, "Oh that Stella . . . always playing a role." He paused to swallow.

Kate paused, too. Could they all be role

players? Was she playing the June Cleaver wife and mother? Was Marlene playing the tough gal with a heart of gold? Was Mary Frances playing the coquette? Was Joe, in his crisp khakis and white linen shirt, playing the sainted husband, still loyal to the dead sinner?

With a wry grin, he continued, "We lived in California for almost three years, then I was assigned to Guam. No way would that woman move there — so that's when she first came up with our married, but separated scheme. We lived apart on and off for years."

"And you agreed to that?" Marlene sounded angry. At what? Or whom? Joe? Stella? Kate couldn't tell.

"Yeah. I loved her. I didn't see how I had much choice." He blushed. "And our reunions were terrific."

Kate stood. "Is dinner ready, Marlene? Let's eat."

Stella's mysterious past went on hold during dinner, as Mary Frances and Marlene regaled Joe with tales of his dead wife's triumphs during her reign as Ocean Vista's condo president. By the time Marlene's pound cake, topped with her million-dollar secret fudge frosting, arrived at the table, a stranger walking in might have thought that four friends had gathered to mourn the death of a fifth.

But the shaky truce ended over coffee when Marlene asked, "When did Stella move to Chicago, Joe?"

Her question was met with what appeared to be a genuinely puzzled expression, complete with an arched white eyebrow. And when Joe spoke, he sounded sad. "Look, other than changing planes at O'Hare, to my knowledge, Stella never stepped foot in Chicago."

Marlene threw up her hands. "But, Joe, Stella told me that you'd died ten years ago in Chicago and that's why she moved to Florida."

"Stella has said a lot of things over the years." His voice caught. "But I'm not dead, am I? And I never lived in Chicago, either. Stella moved to Florida from Bedford Falls, Michigan — near where we'd grown up — and where we'd made one last stab at living together. So clearly some of her stories weren't true."

Kate almost felt sorry for him. But he could be lying. Playing the widower's part. Turning on the tears. Presenting his version of their bizarre relationship. Discrediting the victim. Conning them into trusting him.

Mary Frances, holding Marlene's silver coffeepot, hovered over Joe. "Let me pour you another cup."

Kate's flicker of pity ignited into anger. "After you left the police station, did you get a chance to stop at the funeral parlor? I know you were quite concerned about the cost."

"Gosh, no. After hours of questions, I came directly back here from the police station. Detective Carbone seems to believe that I had something to do with Stella's death. As you all know, I was fishing out in the Atlantic when Stella was killed. What's wrong with that man?"

"You can hardly blame him," Mary Frances snapped, all semblance of flirting forgotten. "Your alibi had enough holes in it to sink your friend's sailboat."

Joe sighed. "Yeah. But my weak alibi somehow seems to be a plus with Carbone, maybe the only asset I have."

And maybe, Kate thought, Joe Sajak was a lot smarter than he sounded.

"Anyway, Carbone's grilling made me nervous, so when I got home, I called Wyndam Oberon to ask if I should hire an attorney. He offered to represent me for now, and if, God forbid, I were to be arrested, he'd recommend a criminal attorney. Then he gave me some good news."

Marlene, helping herself to another piece of cake said, "Do tell."

"I told Wyndam how worried I was about the cost of the funeral." Joe's voice sounded deeper than ever. "Though I wanted the best for Stella, I wondered how I could afford to pay for it. She didn't have a lot of money, you know, no life insurance either, and I sure didn't have much money. Or at least that's what I thought." He smiled broadly. "But now Stella can have a first-class sendoff. Turns out that just last week she'd deposited a cashier's check for two hundred thousand dollars into her checking account."

Marlene dropped her fork. "Two hundred thousand? Where did the money come from?"

Joe said, "Since it was a cashier's check, Wyndam is clueless. Looks like Stella's murder isn't the only mystery we have to solve."

FIFTEEN

Could a copy of that cashier's check have found its way into the obit file that Stella had given to Nancy? Or maybe a receipt? Or a stub that identified its purchaser?

Kate paced her balcony, the fresh ocean breeze and now starry sky doing nothing to soothe her nerves. Ballou, keeping her company, had fallen asleep near the door. She couldn't get that check out of her mind, convinced that a clue, if not connected to the two hundred thousand dollars, then to some other evidence, was in Stella Sajak's folder. Her strong hunch wouldn't let go . . . what time was it anyway? As if in answer to her silent question, the grandfather clock in the living room — inherited from Charlie's aunt — chimed. Eleven p.m. Too late to call Nancy? Probably, Kate thought, heading straight to the phone.

After looking up Nancy Cooper in the condo directory, Kate dialed and got her answering machine. Could the woman still be at work, writing those two articles? Only this morning — though it seemed like a lifetime ago — Kate had jotted down Nancy's office number on the pad next to the telephone.

Nancy picked up on the first ring. "Where are you? I've been waiting —"

"Nancy, it's Kate Kennedy."

"Damn, I'm too busy to talk . . ." Curt. Angry. And something more. Wary? Nervous?

"But —"

"Just a second, Kate." Nancy's voice was muffled. "Who's there? Joe?"

Kate strained to listen. Had Nancy said *Joe?* Or *Yo?* Or *Oh?*

"What are you doing here?" Now Nancy's voice came through loud and clear. She sounded terrified.

A loud, sharp noise, sounding very much like a gunshot, exploded in Kate's ear. Then someone hung up the phone.

Fumbling, frightened beyond reason, Kate scrambled for and found Detective Carbone's number. He wasn't there. In a trembling voice, she left a message then, bordering on hysteria, dialed 911. Frustrated when no one answered, she left another message, then hung up and called Marlene. No answer there either. Kate dashed out of the apartment. She had to get to the Palmetto Beach Gazette Building. Nancy Cooper might still be alive.

As she turned onto the bridge, Kate prayed to Saint Jude and to Charlie, two men that she'd long relied on for help with impossible causes, hoping for the best, but preparing for another body.

Who had walked into Nancy's office?

128

Apparently, not the visitor she'd been expecting.

And where was Marlene when Kate needed her?

Kate glanced north toward David Fry's. Spotlights on the lawn illuminated the yellow exterior and inside lights blazed, seemingly from every nook and cranny. On the dock behind the mansion, huge lanterns made the yacht and the water gleam. Was the master at home? Or had he lit the place up like a Christmas tree to give that impression?

Most of the people on the island side of Palmetto Beach went to bed early, and even the few night owls seldom ventured across to the mainland after 10 p.m. Except for Kate's, there were no cars on Neptune Boulevard. She hit the gas.

Turning right at Federal Highway, she merged into light northbound traffic, passing by the police station. Two patrol cars were in the parking lot; otherwise, all seemed quiet. Had no one listened to her 911 message?

The Gazette Building's parking lot, dark, gloomy, and almost empty, made Kate hesitate, but as Charlie always said, adrenaline fuels fools. She opened her car door, stepped out, and started briskly around to the front of the building. Not a sign of life.

The palm trees swayed in a gentle wind. She jumped as their soft rustling sounds seemed to follow in her footsteps. With a pounding heart — her pulse rate had to be at its all-time high

— Kate forced herself forward.

A dry crackling sound came from behind. Oh God! Something . . . no, someone had stepped on a fallen leaf. She glanced over her shoulder. A dark shadow loomed. Screaming, she stumbled, then spun around and ran for the front door.

Panting, panicked, Kate tried the doorknob. Her sweaty palm made it slippery going. Could it be locked? God, had all the other employees gone home? Shouldn't a newspaper in the process of going to press be open? She caught a whiff of something smoky. Though it had been decades ago on a firing range with Charlie, she hadn't forgotten the smell of a recently discharged gun. As a siren wailed, she felt a cold metal object against the base of her skull. Tires squealed. The front door swung open. Too terrified to turn around, Kate sensed rather than heard her stalker retreat. Stanley Ferris came out of the building, looking befuddled. "What are you doing here, Kate? And what the hell is all the commotion about?"

Kate collapsed in a heap at his feet.

"Are you okay, Mrs. Kennedy? Come on, take a deep breath."

Kate could hear Detective Carbone, but she couldn't open her eyes.

"Doc, you got any smelling salts in that bag?"

"Nick, the people I work on don't require smelling salts."

Such an old-fashioned remedy, Kate thought. Her mother always kept a jar of smelling salts in the house. But since none of the Kennedys had ever passed out — except on occasion, Uncle Mike, after having imbibed too much of her father's bourbon — Kate had tossed the jar after her mother died. She wanted to speak, to assure Detective Carbone that she was fine, but no words came.

A cocoon engulfed her. Warm. Cozy. She couldn't escape. Maybe she didn't want to. So ugly up there. Had the menace with the smoking gun gone? Should she stay down here forever?

"Kate, wake up!" The detective sounded desperate.

"You have no right to hold me, Carbone," Stanley shouted. "I had nothing to do with this!" His strident tone hurt Kate's ears. "I didn't even know about Nancy Cooper until you cops arrived. You're harassing me. Violating my civil rights. Next you'll be dragging me off to the police station like you did Tuesday night. I only went into the Gazette Building because nature called — at my age, when you gotta go, you gotta go — and I knew there was a bathroom on the first floor. Why won't you believe me? Are you crazy? What reason would I have to harm Nancy?"

His shrill voice rose yet another octave. "I'm just an innocent bystander."

An innocent bystander at two murders in two days? Kate opened her eyes.

"Go back into the lobby, Mr. Ferris. Now," Detective Carbone barked. "If you don't sit down and give Officer Jefferson your statement, you'll be sleeping in a cell tonight."

Someone had placed a jacket under Kate's head. She squirmed, then raised her shoulders, struggling to sit up.

"Welcome back." Detective Carbone helped her to a sitting position.

"Nancy Cooper's dead, isn't she? I smelled the gunpowder."

"Is that a confession, Mrs. Kennedy?" Carbone's edgy attitude had resurfaced.

"Hardly. The killer stood behind me and held a gun to my head."

An oval-shaped man with a kind face — probably the "doc" that Nick Carbone had been talking to — took Kate's pulse.

"A little low, but you should be okay. I'm Horatio Harmon, the medical examiner. I haven't seen a live patient in over thirty years. It's a real pleasure. How are you feeling, Mrs. Kennedy?"

"Fine. A little foolish." Kate's voice was weak. "I've never fainted before, but then no one has ever tried to kill me before."

"If you're feeling up to it, I'll drive you home. I'll have someone bring your car back tomorrow morning. But tonight, there are some questions that only you can answer." Nick Carbone took her arm and led her to a late-model Mercedes.

Well, well. What was the salary range for a detective in Palmetto Beach?

Glad to be alive, Kate savored the night air. With the bright moon and balmy breeze, her stalker seemed only a shadowy memory. Almost surreal. Then the truth hit. Hard. Despite her best efforts, Nancy Cooper had been murdered.

She'd barely buckled her seat belt when Carbone said, "You're way too American to be Miss Marple, and you're way too old to be Nancy Drew, so why the hell can't you stay home and let me do my job?"

"How dare you speak to me like that? If either you or the 911 operator had answered my calls, I would have stayed home, but since the Palmetto Beach Police couldn't save that woman, I had to try."

He sighed. "Sorry. It's been a lousy night. About an hour ago, a power outage crippled our 911 system and all the computers. Actually, I'm mad at myself. I moved fast when I got your message. Just not fast enough."

"I'm sorry, too. My night wasn't any better."

"Listen, Kate — er — excuse me, can I call you Kate?"

She nodded, feeling oddly satisfied.

"I'm fifty-nine years old, three years away from any decent retirement. The only detective older than me who's still on the job is Jerry Orbach. And the Palmetto Beach Police Department is no NYPD. If we take our retirement after twenty, twenty-five years, our pensions are worth bupkus. And mostly because of my big mouth, I've made enemies in the current administration. I've been investigating David Fry. Mayor Walters and her council would like me gone — now. Hell, I moved here from Brooklyn over thirty-five years ago, but I'm still considered an alien."

Understanding what he meant, but unsure what to say, Kate nodded again.

"Okay." He sounded gruff and maybe a little embarrassed. "Tell me everything that happened tonight."

Fifteen minutes later, Carbone pulled into Ocean Vista's driveway, and Kate finished telling all, including the cashier's check and her theory about the Stella Sajak folder containing an important clue.

"So you think that Nancy said 'Joe' when the shooter killer walked into her office?"

"Possibly, but I can't swear to it."

"Are you going to walk your dog tonight?"

"No, I took him out earlier. He's probably sound asleep."

"Listen to me," Carbone said, testy as ever.

"Phone that pushy sister-in-law of yours and tell her that starting tomorrow, she has to walk the dog with you. Nancy Cooper called you 'Kate' just as the killer walked into her office. And then someone tried to shoot you. Hardly a coincidence. I don't want you going anywhere alone."

It wasn't until she opened her apartment door and a sleepy Ballou came to greet her that Kate once again wondered where Marlene had disappeared to after dinner.

SIXTEEN

The phone rang, jarring Kate awake. Her alarm clock, which she'd turned off last night, read 9:00 a.m. — the latest she'd slept since Charlie's death. Considering that she hadn't gotten to bed until well after twelve, it must have been a peaceful night, the sheets were barely rumpled.

"Hello." Charlie used to call her morning voice sexy, but to Kate it sounded like a three-pack-a-day-smoker's last rasp.

"Are you still sleeping? Get up! Get up!" Marlene shouted. "The cops just hauled Stanley out of the hot tub and are reading him his rights! I'm on Mary Frances's cell phone. Come on down, you're missing all the fun."

"He'll be gone before I can get dressed. Take notes. I'll see you later."

Kate bolted out of bed, stepping on Ballou — who'd been sleeping next to the bed, and now gave an indignant yelp — grabbed her terry cloth robe, and raced to the balcony.

The blinding morning sun smacked her in the face.

Shading her eyes with her right hand, Kate peered over the concrete ledge. Ballou hovered behind her, waiting for his morning walk. Though she'd never seen the pool so crowded, and a gaggle of sunbathers had clustered around Stanley, once again her balcony provided a great view.

The officer, whom Nick Carbone had referred to last night as Jefferson, spoke to Stanley, then motioned for him to place his hands behind his back.

"But I'm an innocent man!" The half-plea/half-protest echoed above the crowd's buzz.

The cop handcuffed him. Another officer, with a wide wave of his arm, parted the crowd, then led Stanley, dressed in spandex trunks and flip-flops, through it.

Would the police let him stop at his apartment to change? Or would he be booked in his bathing suit?

Kate found herself rooting for the latter.

Kate threw on a caftan Marlene had given her — God, could she be going Florida? — and disobeying Carbone, she took Ballou for a quick walk along A1A. With the police still around, she felt safe.

Back in her kitchen, she put two slices of rye into the toaster and laced her Lipton with a little milk, then thumbed through the *Palmetto Beach Gazette*. She found neither the exposé on David Fry nor Nancy Cooper's big hush-hush scoop. Only Stella's obit had made it to print. So could Fry have shot Nancy to prevent the piece about him from being published? Or to kill the third story? Or both?

As with so many questions in this case, she had no answers.

Kate usually did her best thinking while sipping tea in her Villeroy & Boch white china cup. Charlie had given her the set for their twentieth anniversary, saying, "Use these dishes every day and think of me every time you have a sip of tea." Life, as Charlie's death had proved, was way too short to waste on pottery mugs.

Late last night, worried and wondering where Marlene had gone, Kate had called her. Marlene had been wide awake, watching *Mr. Skeffington* on AMC. Kate thought her former sister-in-law sounded both anxious and pensive. And for a woman whose personal philosophy always had been "what's on your lung is on your tongue" and reflection only what she saw in the mirror, that was most unusual behavior.

Marlene had taken umbrage when Kate questioned where she'd gone after dinner and avoided a direct answer, saying, "Sorry, I didn't check my messages."

When Kate had explained what had happened, Marlene's mood swung from pensive to angry. "Oh God, I'm so sorry, Kate. You know I would have gone with you. Damn, what a night you've had. Carbone is right, you can't go out alone until the killer is caught. Someone wants you dead. And by God, I'm going to find out who that someone is."

But why had Marlene been evasive? Kate spread strawberry preserves on her toast, and shook her head. Was she losing her mind? She certainly didn't suspect Marlene, did she? A white china saucer slipped from her shaky hand, crashing to the floor in smithereens. Tears rolled down her cheeks as she picked up the pieces.

Ballou ran his pink tongue along her ankle. Though Charlie had encouraged the little Westie to jump up — with help — into his lap, and man and dog had enjoyed those sessions of stroking and petting, Kate never wanted the dog on her lap. After Charlie's death, Marlene had been the one who held him, crooning and talking nonsense. Always spoiling him, she'd throw down a treat whenever Ballou and Kate walked past her almost sand-level balcony. If Marlene wasn't there, he'd look up and give a smart yelp, and often as not, she'd appear, bearing goodies.

This morning, feeling very alone and very vulnerable, Kate picked up Ballou, fed him a bit of toast, and talked a little nonsense herself.

And with the Westie's loving response, her self-pity ebbed.

She blew her nose, poured herself another cup of tea, and served Ballou a proper breakfast.

So with Stanley in jail, was it safe to go out on her own? Kate didn't think so. A snake, yes. A murderer, no. Though the thought of Stanley being fingerprinted gave her perverse pleasure, she wondered why Carbone had arrested him.

Ballou was ready for his real walk; maybe Marlene or Mary Frances could join them. Kate stepped onto the balcony. The pool area had emptied out — after all, the show was over — but Mary Frances was sitting alone on a chaise. Good, she'd get down there right away.

As Kate and a frisky Ballou started out the door, the phone rang. Damn, should she answer it and risk missing Mary Frances? A rhetorical question. Had she ever in her life not answered a ringing phone?

"Hello."

"Kate, it's Nick Carbone. Did you hear that Stanley Ferris has been arrested?"

Ballou gave a small, smart yelp, scratching at her legs, as if asking why the delay?

"I caught the show from my balcony." She pushed the dog away. "Look, I know that Stanley was at the scene of the crime and all, but how could he stick a gun in my neck . . . and then walk out the front door?"

"There's a side entrance." Cabone sounded unconvinced.

"But if Stanley had the gun to my head, there wouldn't have been time for him to get

140

around to the side of the building. I felt the cold steel, then bang, he opened the door."

"Okay, you didn't hear this from me." Carbone groaned. "The mayor has been driving the captain crazy, calling every fifteen minutes all night long, pushing for a quick arrest. Season starts the end of this month. She doesn't want the killer on the loose, making the snow birds nervous, sending the tourists scurrying up to Boca Raton. What can I tell you? The captain caved."

"But what you're saying couldn't have happened. You've arrested the wrong man."

"Well, old Doc Harmon says it could have happened. One theory: You never had a gun against your head, sheer terror had triggered your imagination. Or theory number two: Maybe there was a gun against your head, but not at the same time as the door opened and Stanley exited. Maybe you were in such a state of shock that you confused the sequence of events."

"That old quack hadn't seen a live patient in over thirty years. He wouldn't know shock from Shinola." Fury made her voice crackle.

Carbone laughed. "And I haven't heard that expression in over thirty years — though you've cleaned it up some."

"This is an outrage . . ."

"Calm down, Kate. We're only holding Stanley as a material witness in Nancy Cooper's death."

141

"But the cops read him his rights and handcuffed him."

"Yes, we've charged him with Stella's Sajak's murder."

"Oh?" When Carbone didn't answer, she said, "You found something when you searched his apartment, didn't you? I just knew there had to be something in his computer, but I thought it might be porn."

"Look, just to be on the safe side, stay close to home, and when you have to go out, take someone with you, okay?"

"You don't believe that Stanley killed Stella, do you?" Her shout startled Ballou.

"Good-bye, Kate." Carbone hung up.

Mary Frances was closing a beach umbrella when Kate arrived at the pool. "Kate, why didn't you come down? Are you okay? Marlene told me that someone tried to shoot you last night. That's so scary and I'm so frightened." Mary Frances spoke in staccato-like gulps, and her swollen eyes indicated that she'd been crying. "Oh God, do you think Stanley is capable of killing two women and then holding a gun to your head? Could my judgment in men be that bad? I feel so stupid. So gullible. I'm considering going back to the convent. I've decided that South Florida is the Garden of Eden after the snake moved in. How could I have been so flattered by that lying ladies' man?"

Ballou had been tugging on his leash and nipping at Kate's legs all through Mary Frances's monologue.

The oppressive, "hard to catch your breath" heat reminded Kate that only mad dogs and Englishmen go out in the midday sun.

"Why don't you take a walk with us, and I'll tell you why I don't believe that Stanley-the-Snake pointed a gun at me or killed either of those women."

"You don't? But the police . . . and Marlene . . ."

"Where is Marlene?"

"Gone off with Joe Sajak to the funeral parlor. The visiting hours start tonight at seven. He wanted to see Stella before the cremation."

Ballou gave a loud yelp.

Mary Frances grabbed her beach bag. "Come on, Kate, your dog really has to go. And as Stanley always says, when you gotta go, you gotta go."

"His exact words at the scene of the crime, Mary Frances. And in my opinion, Stanley's visit to the men's room is every bit as good an alibi as Joe's solitary sail."

SEVENTEEN

"What do you mean I can't scatter her over the ocean?" Marlene shook her finger in Samuel Adams's face. "That was Stella's last request, and by God, those ashes are going into the Atlantic!"

"Ms. Friedman, I usually handle the traditional burials; cremations are my brother John's specialty. Unfortunately, I wasn't up to snuff on all the rules and regulations governing the disposal of the deceased's remains in the ocean. I do apologize for dispensing misinformation." The little man nervously adjusted the top button on his white polyester jacket.

Damn, Marlene thought, he sounds just like a politician.

They were standing in what Marlene and Kate had dubbed the funeral parlor's Cape Cod Room. The faux fireplace emanated no heat, yet its logs were flickering. Marlene, fascinated, stared at the preprogrammed dancing lights.

It was 87 degrees outside.

Mr. Adams back-stepped, moving out of range of Marlene's index finger and its weapon-like nail, today painted with Revlon's

Fire & Ice. "Now, I'm not saying that some mourners don't stroll out to the end of the Neptune Boulevard Pier and empty their urns into the sea with no questions asked — unless the local fishermen complain — but you can't go scattering ashes on a public beach. What would our Palmetto Beach citizens and the tourists who were swimming nearby think? Not to mention how upsetting it might be for the elderly. You could hire a boat, motor out a bit, and then deposit Mrs. Sajak's ashes in the briny."

Joe, seemingly not listening, opened a large manila envelope and pulled out three photographs. An eight-by-ten sepia of a very young Stella and Joe taken aboard the *Maid of the Mist* in Niagara Falls on their honeymoon. Another of their first grade class, a freckle-faced Joe peering out from behind the mass of dark curls framing Stella's face. The third, a studio-posed color portrait of Stella, circa 1968. Though only in her thirties, gray streaks highlighted her teased bouffant. He handed the photographs to the funeral director. "These are my favorite pictures of my wife. Please put them on a nice table next to her urn."

"I will, Mr. Sajak." Adams spoke softly.

"Why can't I take Stella on her final voyage?" Joe Sajak turned from Samuel Adams to address Marlene in his sad baritone. "My friend's boat is still docked at Pier 66

145

and he won't be back till Monday. Maybe after the memorial service tomorrow morning, you and I and Wyndam can motor out and give Stella the sendoff she deserves."

A less than mollified Marlene, who'd been picturing herself barefoot in a flowing white dress, gliding through the sand and scattering Stella as the bagpiper she'd engaged played "Somewhere Beyond the Sea," shrugged. "I guess that would work."

Samuel Adams beamed. "Splendid. Now, Mr. Sajak, would you like to see the urn that Ms. Friedman and I have chosen to transport your late wife's remains? It's really quite beautiful. From our Persian collection."

"First, I want to say good-bye to my wife. Alone. Where is she?" The widower wasn't much taller than the funeral director, but seemed to tower over Adams.

"Now? Are you sure? We're almost ready to begin the cremation. Remember, Mrs. Sajak has just arrived from the coroner's. We haven't embalmed her or applied any makeup." Adams tittered nervously. "It's not as if we thought anyone would be seeing her prior to . . ."

"I'm going to see her. Now." Joe sounded determined.

"Well," Adams huffed, "it won't be pleasant."

"Death never is. Take me to my wife."

Adams looked at Marlene. "Are you joining us, Ms. Friedman?"

She hesitated. Though she would like to have seen Joe's reaction when he viewed the body, he'd said, "Alone," and sounded as if he meant it. "No, I'll wait here." Sitting down on the red, cut-velvet settee, she checked for an ashtray. "Can I smoke?"

"Sorry, Ms. Friedman," Adams said. "As you may recall from when we made Mrs. Sajak's arrangements, this is a smoke-free funeral parlor. You can have a cigarette out back where the hearses are parked."

An hour later, Marlene and Joe were in her convertible, heading for the nearest bar. She'd passed on being present at the actual cremation, but Joe had insisted on witnessing it and the ordeal had left him visibly shaken.

"The Dew Drop Inn is on Federal Highway, near Town Hall," Marlene said, "and the bartender makes a mean martini."

"That's fine with me." Joe's deep baritone had become a hoarse whisper.

But Marlene knew better; nothing was fine, and the man looked like death walking. For once in her life, she didn't know what to say, so probably to Joe's relief, she turned left and drove the rest of the way in silence.

At a little after one, exiting the hot bright sunshine and entering the cool, dark bar seemed a sinful pleasure. The burgers, grilling on an open flame, smelled delicious, the patrons looked happy, and the cocktails, served straight up in chilled glasses, were perfect. Marlene, comfortable in her natural habitat, settled onto the bar stool and took a sip of her drink, feeling better already.

She raised her glass. "To Stella."

Joe nodded. "May she rest in peace." He wiped his eyes, then drained most of his martini. "How the hell can you have a viewing when there's only a pile of ashes packed in an urn?"

Marlene remembered how she'd said almost those exact words to Kate on Wednesday.

Either Sajak was the world's best con man or a brokenhearted husband. Marlene, having no clue which, suggested that they order another round of drinks and a couple of cheeseburgers. With fries.

The bartender took their order, saying that they could eat at the bar. Joe, apparently not too grief-stricken to eat, asked for a side of onion rings.

Then Marlene, fortified by the gin yet unable to think of a tactful way to phrase the question that had been driving her crazy — subtlety not her strong suit — finally blurted out, "So who do you think gave Stella that two-hundred-thousand-dollar cashier's check?"

Joe laughed, but even his laughter sounded sad. Or was that part of his act? "I'm more curious about why? What had Stella been up to?"

"Blackmail?" Damn! Her mother always said that Marlene never had an unspoken thought. If only she could bite back her words, but they hung out there, cold and ugly, as Joe, in one gulp, swallowed the rest of his martini.

"I was thinking more along the lines of Stella selling the family jewels. My Aunt Erma left her a diamond brooch and a fine-looking emerald ring. Stella never wore them, said they were old-fashioned and gaudy, but I figured they might be valuable." He speared his olive. "Is there something you know that I don't?"

Marlene fumbled, feeling foolish. "Well, blackmail came to mind; that's quite a chunk of change . . ."

David Fry, catching her completely off guard, perched on the bar stool next to her. "Hello, Ms. Friedman, and how are you today? I understand that Ocean Vista's vice-president has been arrested for Stella Sajak's murder." He shook his head. "Pity. There goes the neighborhood."

Marlene forced a smile, then motioned toward Joe. "Allow me to introduce you to Joe Sajak, Stella's husband. Or I should say, her widower. Joe, this is David Fry, the man that Stella wanted to throw to the lions. Or at least out of town."

Extending his hand to Joe, David Fry, properly respectful yet smooth as silk stockings, said, "I'm so sorry for your loss, Mr. Sajak. Your wife was a worthy adversary, and though we had different visions for Palmetto Beach, I assure you our difference would have been settled in Town Hall, not the Coliseum."

A flurry of excitement in the dining area captured Marlene's attention. A fawning young waiter was seating a party of four at a window table, not that Federal Highway afforded much of a view. Fancy that: the mayor and her three stooges.

Marlene gestured toward the window table and said to Fry, "I think your luncheon companions have arrived."

"So I see." He smiled, icy charm intact. "Please excuse me, Ms. Friedman. Business before pleasure, but I haven't forgotten that I owe you and Mrs. Kennedy a drink."

"And dinner."

David Fry actually bowed, briefly to be sure, but nonetheless a bow. "And certainly, dinner it is. Sometime after the funeral, of course." He turned back to Joe. "Again, my sincere sympathy. I'll see both of you this evening."

As Fry sat next to the mayor, Joe said, "Who's that blonde? She looks like a movie star or —"

"Palmetto Beach's mayor," Marlene snapped. "She's an attractive woman, but I wouldn't go so far as to say that she looks like a movie star."

150

Joe kept staring at Brenda Walters, appearing absolutely mesmerized.

Only the arrival of the bartender, balancing two huge plates of cheeseburgers, fries, and onion rings, and announcing, "Here we go, the best food in Broward County," broke Joe's concentration.

Back at Ocean Vista, Joe, saying he had a lot of phone calls to make and paperwork to take care of, went up to Stella's — well, his apartment, Marlene begrudgingly thought. She walked over to the reception desk and asked Miss Mitford, who looked bleaker than usual in head-to-toe olive drab, to buzz Kate's condo.

"Mrs. Kennedy isn't here, Mrs. Friedman."

Over the years, Marlene had tried, but failed, to get Miss Mitford to address her as Ms.

"She went off somewhere with Miss Costello."

Marlene felt a pang that she readily identified as jealousy, but she would be damned if she'd ask any more questions.

"I do have a message for you, Mrs. Friedman."

"Yes. From Kate?" Guilt and fear made her voice shake.

"No, that newsboy, Timmy, called. The one who'd brought the note for Mrs. Sajak. He knew you lived in Ocean Vista, but couldn't remember your last name, so he called Information and got the number for the front desk."

"My God . . . when did he call? What did he say?"

"About an hour ago. And he didn't say much of anything, just gave me a phone number up in Palm Beach County for you to call." She handed a scrap of paper to Marlene. "He sounded scared." She smiled as if pleased by that thought. "Naturally I called Detective Carbone right away. So with any luck, Timmy might be in custody by now."

EIGHTEEN

"I have to get out of Palmetto Beach." Mary Frances sounded as if someone were strangling her. "I can't stop thinking about Stanley and what a fool I've been."

Kate, who'd been listening to some version of that lament during their entire walk to the pier and back, patted her hand.

They'd reached Marlene's balcony, which hung low over the beach and the north side of the swimming pool. As usual, Ballou had stopped to bark — a happy, hopeful yelp — his eyes fixated on the balcony like a canine Romeo, willing Marlene to appear.

"Give it up, Ballou." Kate yanked the leash. "She's gone off with another guy. No treats today."

Mary Frances smiled. "The not-so-merry widower, yet another suspect, right? I'm rooting for either Sajak or Fry to be the murderer, but God forgive me, I still want Stanley to suffer."

Kate, feeling a bit ashamed of herself, admitted, "My exact sentiments."

"My favorite author is signing at Murder at Del Ray Beach, my favorite bookstore, this afternoon. Do you like mysteries?"

Mary Frances's segue from real to fictional murder puzzled Kate. "I love them — though not the one we're in the middle of — I cut my teeth on Agatha Christie and Rex Stout."

"So, what do you say, Kate? Want to drive up A1A, grab a late lunch, and meet Sue Henry?"

"Does she have a book out?"

"*The Serpents Trail*; it's the first in her new series. Let's blow this burg. We deserve an afternoon off, and besides, Marlene has absolutely refused to accept my help tonight or for tomorrow morning's service, though God knows I've offered and I'm an expert on wakes, hymns, and flower arrangements. Come on, we'll be back in plenty of time for Stella's visitation."

Kate, who hadn't been in a bookstore since Charlie died, smiled, remembering how much she loved them. "Okay."

"Meet me in my apartment in thirty minutes. It's number 720. Go down to the lobby and take the south elevator. I have something I want to show you."

"And this is the dance studio, where I perfect my tango." Mary Frances, pretty in pink capris and a pink and white checked top, tied at the waist, was taking Kate, in khakis and a T-shirt, on a tour of her small one-bedroom condo: an immaculate and amazing 1,000 square feet.

154

"You turned your bedroom into a dance studio?" Kate stared at the raised parquet floor, the ballet barre, the sound system, the three mirrored walls, the fourth covered with clothes racks, filled with colorful costumes, and at the baskets containing castanets, and the open shoe boxes, lined up like soldiers, holding sexy high-heel pumps that matched the costumes and the castanets. How had Mary Frances ever convinced the board to go for this?

"Isn't it wonderful? A competitive dancer must rehearse. I just finished arranging the shoes late last night."

"Where do you sleep?"

Mary Frances winked. "I'll just bet you thought my Murphy bed was an armoire. Everyone does. Let's go back into the living room, I'll show you how it works."

Swinging open the two doors of what, indeed, appeared to be an armoire, Mary Frances revealed a double bed then, with one hand, had it out of the closet and on the floor. On either side of the Murphy bed/armoire, floor-to-ceiling bookcases covered the rest of the wall; they were filled with dolls. All kinds of dolls, from Barbie, in every conceivable incarnation, to Raggedy Ann, to the six wives of Henry the VIII.

Kate glanced around the room: sparse. The ubiquitous off-white couch, two small wing chairs covered in a violet-patterned chintz, a white Formica coffee table — topped with neat stacks of *Cosmopolitan* and *Glamour* magazines, and several mystery paperbacks — and two matching Formica end tables. Other than a small entertainment center, holding a TV, a VCR, and a CD player, built-in bookcases — all displaying dolls — took up every inch of the remaining wall space. Most of the dolls wore elaborate, obviously expensive, outfits, and were behind glass doors.

"Beautiful, aren't they?" Mary Frances said. "I think of them as my children."

Did she sound defensive? Kate tried to keep her expression neutral and to hide her . . . what? Surprise? Shock? Distaste?

"I'm still a virgin, you know."

That was more information than Kate needed. Or was it? If she could come up with the right questions, maybe this childlike side of Mary Frances might even, if inadvertently, provide some answers.

Kate drove her old Chevy Impala along A1A on Millionaires Row in Highland Beach, thinking that with yachts on her left, and mansions on her right, complete with tennis courts and leafy green trees on lawns that led to the ocean, she could be in Southampton.

"I feel so sorry about Nancy," Kate said. "Did you know her well?"

"Well, she was a member of our lonely Hearts club, so I saw her once a week, but no, I wouldn't say I knew her well." Mary Frances seemed to measure her words. "A really good card player. She and Stella almost never wound up with the Queen of Spades . . . that drove Marlene crazy. Nancy, like most reporters, asked a lot of questions, but never said very much about herself." Mary Frances ran her fingers through her red curls. "I've been wondering two things. A — what did Nancy stumble onto? And B — how did the killer know that she'd discovered something?"

The child in Mary Frances must have stayed home with the dolls.

"Nancy's piece about Fry never made today's paper. Strange, isn't it? And what about the obit? Could she have found something in Stella's papers that led her to the killer?"

"I guess anything's possible. But Nancy had all that stuff for months." Mary Frances paused. Kate could almost hear her thinking. "Unless . . ."

"Unless what?"

"Maybe — much more recently — Stella made a slip about her past and then, after her murder, that slip led Nancy to her killer."

"But Stella tried so hard to hide her past. Telling everyone that her husband had died, that she'd lived in Chicago, that she'd attended Northwestern. All lies."

"It's tough to play a part every day, Kate.

157

Even the best actresses can forget their lines . . . or say something that's not in the script."

Mary Frances's words jogged Kate's memory, just as she was forced to inch right to allow a southbound Mercedes, whose driver had drifted across the line, to pass by.

And while concentrating on her driving, the chance to retrieve her lost memory had passed by, too.

They rode in silence through Deerfield Beach and past the Boca Raton condominiums with their fancy French names and prices to match, then chatted about mystery books and their favorite authors, putting any conversation about real murders on hold.

The drive up A1A, though not as picturesque as the Riviera or as breathtakingly awesome as Big Sur, had its own charms. The Atlantic, often only a few feet away from the passenger side window, seemed so much more accessible than either the Mediterranean or the Pacific. Never more so than in Del Ray Beach, where A1A was literally steps from the ocean.

"Make a left here on Atlantic Avenue," Mary Frances said.

Kate laughed. "If I made a right, we'd be in the sand."

The cobblestone street, dotted with ethnic restaurants, sophisticated shops, and pastel art galleries appealed to Kate. Downtown Del Ray had been charmingly restored. She felt as if she were on the verge of an adventure, a feeling that she hadn't had since Charlie died.

"Are we going to eat in one of these places?" Kate was hungry.

"No . . . We're going to take a sentimental journey. Turn left on Federal Highway."

"Everybody loves somebody sometime." The words still made Kate shiver. What a crush she'd had on Dino. Now all these decades later, his voice, emanating from the juke box on their table, still brought goose bumps. Or maybe it was the diner's air-conditioning.

A ponytailed fifty-something waitress, wearing a poodle skirt, brought their chocolate malteds.

Mary Frances clicked her glass against Kate's. "What were you doing in 1960?"

"Expecting my first child. Jackie was pregnant with John John and I was pregnant with Kevin." Kate smiled. "A new decade and a new life. I think that might have been the happiest year of my life." She sipped the thick malted. "What about you?"

"I graduated from All Hallows High School and entered the convent. Mostly I was scrubbing floors or failing Latin. I missed my parents and my little sisters, but I wasn't allowed to see any of my family that first

Christmas. Definitely *not* the happiest year of my life."

"Did things get better?"

"Oh, yes, I had a lot of happy productive years as a nun, but —"

"Quick, Mary Frances, look out the window at that man talking on the pay phone."

Mary Frances craned her neck. "So?"

"It's Timmy. He shaved and showered and has on new clothes, but that's Timmy."

"You mean the missing newsboy?"

"Yes!"

"Who's that man standing next to him? He looks familiar." Mary Frances glanced from the window to Kate, then back again.

Kate peered over the juke box. "I can't see his face."

"Wait . . . he's turning this way. Oh my God, Kate! That's Wyndam Oberon!"

NINETEEN

Kate knocked over her malted as she raced for the diner's front door, with Mary Frances right behind her.

"Hey," the ponytailed waitress yelled, "are you two ladies skipping on the check?"

"We'll be back," Kate called over her shoulder as she dashed through the door, and took a left toward the pay phone. "Timmy," she yelled, barreling by Wyndam Oberon, who jumped out of her path. Marlene had described him well; he did look like Clarence in *It's a Wonderful Life*.

Timmy, who'd just hung up the phone, ran.

Kate ran after him, praying that Mary Frances would detain Oberon. Halfway down the block, Timmy darted into Federal Highway's oncoming traffic, leaving Kate breathless on the curb. She watched as he kept running, dodging cars, then heading east toward the ocean. By the time the light turned green, Timmy had vanished.

Crushed, a still panting Kate walked back toward the pay phone, where Mary Frances had planted both her hands firmly on Wyndam Oberon's shoulders.

"Woman, have you lost your mind?" Wyndam wiggled and squirmed, but couldn't loosen her grip. Mary Frances, employing what looked like a graceful tango arm movement, shoved him against the phone stand. With her strong muscular upper arms, her right knee wedged in his groin, and her in-your-face attitude, the overweight, out-of-shape attorney didn't have a chance.

Several of the diner's patrons had come out to see the show; others pressed their noses to the windows. Rubbernecks slowed traffic — just a tad too late to do Kate any good.

The ponytailed waitress stood a foot or so behind Mary Frances, waving their bill and shouting, "Hey, you check-jumper, let go of Mr. Oberon, he's one of our best customers."

"Have you lost your mind, Miss Costello?" Wyndam sounded more frightened than angry. "I'll have you arrested for assault!"

Even his threat fell flat. What was really going on here?

"You allowed a witness in Stella Sajak's murder to get away." Kate could see the tension in Mary Frances's knuckles. "I'd call that aiding and abetting." Perry Mason couldn't have done better. "What were you doing with Timmy in the first place? Did you hire him to deliver that note to Stella on the afternoon of her murder?"

An audible *oooh* came from the crowd.

Kate reevaluated: Mary Frances's cross-examination was much more aggressive than Perry's.

"I never saw that man before in my life." Wyndam Oberon's drawl drooped like a weeping willow. "My cell phone died. I was waiting to use the pay phone when he ran, and that lady" — Oberon jerked his head toward Kate — "chased after him, and then you attacked me." Indignation crept into his voice. "Now get your hands off me, woman!"

"Search him, Kate. Find his cell phone and see if it's working."

A man, whom Kate recognized as the diner's cashier, stepped out of the crowd and closed in on Mary Frances. As Kate threw herself between Mary Frances and the cashier, Oberon somehow managed to reach into his jacket pocket and yank out his cell phone. Kate strained her arm, trying to intercept, but it fell to the pavement. Or had Oberon dropped it?

The pay phone rang. Everyone froze. As in Statue — a game Kate hadn't played in almost sixty years, where one player would yell "Freeze!" and the other players would stop wherever they were and whatever they were doing and turn into statues.

On the second ring, Kate, her hand shaking, picked up the phone and, almost whispering, said, "Hello . . ."

"Who is this?" A shout, not a whisper.

Oh my God! She must have entered the

twilight zone. The caller was Nick Carbone.

A police siren jolted her back to reality.

"So do you want the hot fudge minisundae or not?" The ponytailed waitress had gone off duty, and her replacement, an elderly redhead, who'd missed most of the commotion, wasn't *quite* treating them like the enemy.

After almost two hours of sitting through in-person interviews with a Del Ray detective, and separate phone interviews with an "angry at both of them" Detective Carbone, and threats of charges being pressed by Wyndam Oberon, and no proof of anything, since the attorney claimed that the fall had "jarred something" in the cell phone, causing it to work again, Kate and Mary Frances finally were finishing lunch.

Mary Frances nodded at the waitress. "Yes, please bring us two sundaes and two cups of tea. And you can clear these plates."

Kate couldn't believe how quickly they'd devoured their BLTs with slaw and fries.

"You didn't buy that garbage that Oberon was feeding to the police, did you?" Mary Frances pulled out a small mirror and checked her teeth.

Kate shook her head. "No way, Wonder Woman. And thanks again, you were marvelous. Look, Timmy called Ocean Vista and left that pay phone's number and, obviously, he'd been waiting for Marlene to call him back. Oberon *had* to be waiting there with him. I don't believe in coincidences and I know that Nick Carbone doesn't either." Kate shoved the Marlene-Timmy connection to the back of her mind.

"But we can't prove that the cell phone . . ."

"There's a connection between Timmy and Wyndam Oberon and I'm going to find it."

"Didn't Detective Carbone tell us to go home and stay there?"

Kate, suddenly remembering one of Charlie's cases, glanced at her watch. "Let's eat our sundaes and get out of here, Mary Frances. I'm really sorry we missed the signing, but I want to stop at the Neptune Inn on the way home. I need to ask the owner about Timmy."

"So does anyone know where Stella went after she read the note that he'd delivered? Maybe whatever happened after he'd left the lobby on Tuesday afternoon is why she wound up on the beach that night."

"You're ahead of me." Kate smiled. This gal was sharp. "I plan to do a timeline on Stella, too. I'm sure Carbone checked out where she went, and I'm sure the note had something to do with her murder." Why *hadn't* either she or Marlene followed up on where Stella had gone?

"You're investigating this case for real, aren't you? No wonder the killer tried to shoot you."

"Well . . ."

Mary Frances, who'd devoured her sundae in three bites, put twenty dollars on the table. "Come on, let's take I-95 back, we'll get there faster."

Kate, though nervous about driving on I-95, agreed. It couldn't be worse than the Long Island Expressway.

It was. By Boca, Kate wished that she could trade seats with Mary Frances. The Florida drivers honked even more often than New Yorkers, exceeded the speed limits, and seemed to change lanes every sixty seconds.

Mary Frances had returned to complaining about Stanley while professing his innocence. Between the traffic and the tirade, and the fat heavy lunch, Kate's mood was sour.

"Look, Mary Frances, I think we've eliminated Stanley as a suspect, and as a topic of conversation. Now I'd like to ask you a question."

"When you've never had a boyfriend, Kate, even someone like Stanley Ferris seems appealing. He told me that I'm lovely."

Kate sighed. "And you are. Far too lovely and far too smart for such a sleazy man." She turned the wheel sharply to avoid a close encounter with an overly aggressive lane changer.

"Okay." Mary Frances sounded more upbeat. "Ask away."

"On our way up to Del Ray, you compared

Stella to an actress who'd forgotten her lines, and that insight jogged my memory, and a senior moment I've been trying to recall almost surfaced. But then I had to move over to let that road-hogging Mercedes pass and —"

"Oh, I know all about senior moments. You saw how small my apartment is . . . yet sometimes, I walk into the kitchen and have no idea why I'm there, so I trot back into the living room, and then remember what I'd wanted from the kitchen."

"Been there, done that . . . a lot." Kate chuckled. "But this seems different, almost as if I've blocked it on purpose. I know that we were at Town Hall after the meeting, and Stella and the mayor were talking, and David Fry was standing there, looking superior, and Stanley had his arms draped —"

"Around Marlene and Stella." Mary Frances sniffed. "That awful man, flirting his way through the crowd, when he had a date with me that night. And to think I went to meet him on the beach despite his bad behavior."

Damn! Why had Kate said that about Stanley, getting Mary Frances all riled up again? Because it might be connected to her senior moment?

"Forget about Stanley, Mary Frances. I need you to focus. As we were leaving Town Hall, did Stella forget her lines? Say something out of character? Something not in her script?"

"Sorry, Kate, if she did, I don't re-member." Mary Frances hesitated. "But there were other times. Stanley always said that, for a gal from Chicago, Stella knew nothing about the White Sox."

Kate clutched the wheel as the driver in front of her changed lanes without signaling.

"Well, no wonder. According to Joe Sajak, Stella never even visited Chicago."

"Ah, yes, Joe Sajak, our grieving widower, the man who called Wyndam Oberon for advice and counsel when he was afraid that the police might arrest him."

TWENTY

"If you can't drink, smoke, or dance, I don't want to be there."

Kate and Mary Frances were seated at the bar in the Neptune Inn. It was four-thirty, well into the cocktail hour in Palmetto Beach, where most residents dined out on early-bird schedules that often ended before six.

Two old ladies — old by South Florida standards being anyone ten years your senior — were drinking Manhattans and discussing the shortcomings of the Methodist retirement home in Fort Lauderdale.

Though the stock behind the bar was even scarcer than the patrons, Herb Wagner had several bottles of rye and vermouth left on the shelves, along with a lone jar of maraschino cherries. Four of Herb's five other customers were drinking Manhattans. Figuring, when in an about-to-be-demolished bar, do as the regulars do, Kate ordered a Manhattan. Mary Frances, much to Herb's amusement, asked for a Scarlett O'Hara.

"You've never been here before, have you?" Herb gazed at Mary Frances with the eye of a happily married man who still appreciated an attractive woman — what Charlie had called window-shopping.

Recalling that only yesterday he'd looked at her the same way, Kate smiled, "This is Mary Frances Costello, another Ocean Vista resident."

Herb wiped his hand on his apron, then extended it to Mary Frances. "A real pleasure. You girls be careful over there. First Stella, now Nancy Cooper. Ugly business."

One of the Manhattan cocktail–drinking ladies, who was wearing a smart peach pants suit, said, "If you ask me, a serial killer is working his way through your building, targeting women owners. The cops have the wrong man. Stanley Ferris is no killer; he doesn't have the balls."

Mary Frances whirled around on her bar stool. "Do you know Stanley Ferris?"

The second old lady said, "I made a vow never to wear lavender; they line caskets in lavender."

"Stanley and I dated about ten years ago," the first lady said, completely ignoring her friend's non sequitur. "Great dancer. Lousy lover. My name is Jeanette Nelson." She gestured to her friend, "This is Mildred Green."

"I'm Kate Kennedy . . ."

"And I'm Mary Frances Costello." Her voice caught. "I might be the last date that Stanley will ever have."

Mary Frances's frankness surprised Kate.

Mildred had Ivory soap white hair wrapped into a loose chignon, and she wore a gauzy white caftan. She turned to Mary Frances and snorted. "Of all Jeanette's boyfriends, the dancing dentist won the prize for most dreadful, and trust me, they were a motley lot. Did I tell you that I never wear lavender?"

"The Broward County Tango Champion!" Jeanette smiled. "What an honor to meet you, Mary Frances. I was third runner-up in this year's Cha Cha competition, but we danced on different nights and never met. Of course, I read all about how you were there on the beach when Stanley stumbled over Stella's body. Believe me, you're lucky not to be planning a second date with that loser. And with all due respect to your murdered neighbor, Stella Sajak wasn't one of my favorite people — a bossy busybody, wasn't she? Still you won't hear me speaking ill of the dead."

Intrigued, Kate asked, "Have you stayed friendly with Stanley?"

"Well, I'm not going to be visiting him in jail now, am I? But I did have a dance with him at Ireland's Inn last night." Jeanette stabbed her Manhattan-soaked cherry with a stirrer and carefully lifted it to her mouth.

"Do you know what time he left there?" Kate asked, wondering if Stanley had planned to meet someone.

"Yes. Didn't I tell Detective Carbone that Stanley took off, rather abruptly, around ten forty-five, in plenty of time to drive up to the Gazette Building in Palmetto Beach and hold a gun to that poor woman's head." Jeanette snapped the stirrer in half. "I also assured the detective that Stanley wasn't killer material and the cops should keep on looking."

Biting her lip to prevent a grin, Kate thought Carbone must have loved that.

"Kate's the woman who had the gun at her head," Mary Frances said. "Maybe Stanley *is* innocent, but his presence at two murder scenes has persuaded the Palmetto Beach Police Department otherwise."

"My God, Kate!" Jeanette sounded outraged. "What a fright that must have been."

Kate nodded. "Yes. For the first time in my life, I actually fainted." She took another sip of her Manhattan, the alcohol soothing her nerves. She considered ordering a second, but more than one drink wreaked havoc with her stomach. "Tell me, Jeanette, what kind of mood was Stanley in last night? Did he say anything about Stella's murder?"

"No, but he seemed jumpy. Off center. Usually his samba is smoother than a sixteen-year-old girl's stomach, but last night he kept stepping on my big toe. It still hurts." Jeanette stuck out her left foot, shod in a peach leather sandal the exact shade of her pants suit. The big toe appeared seriously swollen. "His mind wasn't on the dance floor, that's for sure."

Kate remembered how Stanley had invited her to go dancing at Ireland's Inn last night, and with the memory came an involuntary shudder. "So he didn't have a date?"

"No. At first, he seemed a little sheepish about being out dancing — what with Stella being so recently dead and all — but as soon as the music started, he seemed to get over that. Guilt's not Stanley's style. Still he was stewing over something. And just before he left, he was off whispering in a corner with a big brassy blonde — kind of a Mae West type — I think she lives in Ocean Vista, too."

"Marlene?" Kate stammered, looking at Mary Frances.

"Yes. That's her name." Jeanette pounded the bar. "Another aggressive —"

"Marlene Friedman was at Ireland's Inn last night?" Mary Frances sounded as crazed as Kate felt. "We'd been to her house for dinner. What time did she get there?"

"I couldn't tell you. Sorry I called her brassy, I didn't know she was a friend of yours. Let's see — the bar was packed — I spotted Marlene with Stanley, then he left. And as I say, that was around ten forty-five. Eleven at the latest."

"I never wear lavender," Mildred said.

No one responded, but she didn't seem to notice as she flagged Herb and ordered another Manhattan.

173

"Make that two, Herb." Jeanette pulled out a pack of Virginia Slims and lit up.

Kate found her voice. "Did Marlene leave with Stanley?"

"I don't think so," Jeanette said, "but I don't recall seeing her after he'd gone."

Mary Frances, backing away from the smoke, said, "How well did you know Stella Sajak?" She twisted a red curl. Kate had noticed that Mary Frances seemed to do that whenever she was concentrating. Or nervous. Or maybe when trying to veer the conversation away from Marlene?

"Stella was the one who tried to change the bingo rules at the Senior Center," Mildred said. "Came on like a union organizer, didn't she, Jeanette?"

Mary Frances laughed. "That sounds like Stella."

"Did I mention that I never wear lavender? Will her casket be lined in lavender?"

Kate, tempted to explain that Stella wouldn't be in a casket, decided not to go there. Yet she marveled at Mildred's thought patterns, which leapt between logic and lunacy.

"I used to see her at the Senior Center and, occasionally, at Ireland's, but I can't say I knew her." Jeanette shrugged. "I wonder if anyone really knew Stella."

Kate, reeling about Marlene and wanting to tread easily with Mary Frances's feelings, was certain that she'd stumbled onto something.

"Did Stella ever come to Ireland's Inn with Stanley?"

"No. She'd have a dance or two with him, but nothing more. Stanley's ex-girlfriends are legion, but Stella remained a singleton. Came alone. Went home alone. For a woman who was always telling everyone else what to do, she seldom spoke about herself. And she never got close to anyone."

"So Stella never dated Stanley?" Mary Frances raised her voice.

Jeanette smiled, forming deep crinkles around her shrewd blue eyes. "She was too smart to fall for Stanley's line. I just wish that I'd been as smart."

Mary Frances flinched. "Herb, I'd like another Scarlett O'Hara."

Kate, more than ready to address the real reason why she and Mary Frances had dropped by the Neptune Inn, said, "Herb, this is important: When Timmy had that last martini here last Tuesday, did he appear to be waiting for anyone? Or speak to anyone? Or use the phone booth?"

Herb shook his head, his heavy jowls swinging slowly from side to side, then flopping back into place. "Not that I remember." Looking deep in thought, he mixed grenadine with Southern Comfort, stirred, handed the cocktail to Mary Frances, then gave Kate his full attention. "I didn't see Timmy talking to anyone other than me. We were almost empty, so I would have noticed."

"You mean Timmy, the newsboy?" Jeanette jumped in, her voice high-pitched and excited. "Last Tuesday afternoon, right? That was the last time I saw him. He just disappeared, you know."

"I know," Kate said, "and I'm trying to find out why."

Those shrewd blue eyes met and held Kate's. "What's it to you?"

"I'm convinced that Timmy has information about Stella's murder. Like you, I don't think Stanley killed either Stella or Nancy and I want to find out who did."

Jeanette nodded. "So we're on the same page, then?"

"Yes," Kate said, "I believe we are." She liked this spunky older woman.

"Well, I don't understand how Timmy's going missing could be connected to Stella's murder, but I can tell you that he met someone on Tuesday afternoon. Not here in the bar — out on the pier. I arrived a little after four and the pier was deserted, except for two men down at the far end, chatting away like old pals, their heads close together. Timmy was one . . ."

"And the other?" Kate was breathless.

Jeanette grinned. "That overstuffed turkey, Wyndam Oberon."

TWENTY-ONE

Circus clowns came to mind as Mary Frances Costello, Jeanette Nelson, and Mildred Green squeezed into Mildred's Miata. The thought of Mildred driving scared Kate and she could see that Mary Frances was less than thrilled to be relegated to the car's minuscule back seat already filled with Lord & Taylor shopping bags.

The three women were heading over to the Palmetto Beach Police Station.

Kate had called Detective Carbone from the Neptune Inn, telling him that Wyndam Oberon had, indeed, known Timmy, and that she had a witness to prove it. She then put Jeanette Nelson on the phone. Carbone had requested Jeanette to come in and give a statement about Timmy's conversation with Oberon on the same day that Timmy had delivered a note to Stella, told Herb Wagner how he'd come into money, and then vanished.

Oberon's and Timmy's four o'clock meeting on the pier on Tuesday was all the more intriguing, considering that this very afternoon the attorney had lied to both the Del Ray and Palmetto Beach Police, denying that he'd ever known the newsboy.

Kate, who had to go home and walk Ballou, sincerely regretted that she couldn't accompany the ladies, if only to hear Mildred Green chat up Nick Carbone.

Jeanette stuck her head out the passenger side window. "Did I tell you that Wyndam's wife ran off with the pool boy back in '88? Can't say that I blame her; the woman certainly wasn't getting any sex from her husband." She winked at Kate. "And I can testify to that!"

Mildred hit the gas and the Miata sped off, causing one hapless A1A beachgoer to drop his umbrella as he jumped out of its way.

As Kate opened her car door, she chuckled. No question about it, Carbone would get interesting answers and wild opinions from Jeanette. Not to mention Mildred's lavender phobia. Humph. Served him right. Wyndam Oberon had been lying through his false teeth and might even be a murderer, but Carbone hadn't even bothered to thank Kate for her detective work.

Ballou, ecstatic to see Kate, nipped and yelped and licked, making their exit strategy difficult, but she finally managed to secure his leash, grab a small bottle of Evian, check her messages, and get him out the door.

Marlene had left two messages indicating that she was worried about Kate and asking

178

her to call as soon as she returned.

She'd deal with that later. Kate had two questions for her sister-in-law. Why had Marlene gone to Ireland's Inn last night? And more importantly, why had she tried to cover up that outing with a lie of omission? She wanted to hear those answers face-to-face.

Kate crossed the lobby, eliciting a frown from Miss Mitford. Didn't that woman ever go off duty? Here it was five-thirty on a Friday night and she was still at her post. Since dogs weren't permitted to walk through the lobby — one of the condo's most frequently violated rules — Kate carried Ballou, obeying the letter of the law, but judging from the expression on the sentinel's face, violating the spirit.

An amazing array of gilt and marble adorned the inside of the front doors.

"Gaudy," she'd told Charlie.

"Impressive," he'd said, "like the Roman baths."

"More John Gotti than Julius Caesar." She'd made him laugh.

Outside, a warm breeze was accompanied by the smell of salt mixed with jasmine. Kate walked south along A1A. On the beach, she might have run into neighbors and, if she'd taken her usual route, north toward the pier, Ballou would have done his Romeo bit under

Marlene's balcony. Kate didn't want to talk to anyone. She needed to think. And she didn't have much time — Stella's visitation started at seven.

Going through Charlie's files yesterday morning, she'd started with the folder marked: JULY '76. The United States of America's bicentennial summer. The summer that Charlie and Kate had celebrated their seventeenth wedding anniversary. And the summer that Charlie had worked on the biggest — and most difficult — case of his career.

They'd married on the Fourth of July. Charlie had chosen the date, saying they would always celebrate with fireworks and that he would never forget his anniversary. And he never did. At a backyard picnic, she'd find a gold bracelet in a scoop of watermelon, or a plane would fly by with sky writing in its wake that read: HAPPY ANNIVERSARY, KATE.

On July 4, 1976, as the big ships had proudly sailed into New York Harbor and red, white, and blue fireworks lit up the heavens, Kate and Charlie had stood, arms entwined on the deck of a friend's sloop, watching the boat parade. He'd kissed her cheek and whispered, "So how do you like this year's present?"

The most romantic night of her life hadn't been on her honeymoon, or even on a star-filled evening with Jack Simon during that torrid summer of 1957, when Kate had gambled on love and lost. The most romantic night ever — and yes, the best sex ever — of her life had happened on July 4, 1976, while celebrating her seventeenth wedding anniversary at the Plaza Hotel.

God, how she missed Charlie.

And later that night, while snuggling, his pillow talk had been about homicide. Kate, as an avid murder mystery fan, enjoyed their postcoital chatter almost as much as the sex.

Charlie's case had involved an errant Park Avenue husband, his seemingly faithful wife, his daughter by a former marriage — a Radio City Rockette — who resented her stepmother, and a rather dashing attorney who'd drawn up the couple's will and was rumored to be interested in the wife.

When the wife's body turned up in a garbage can in the alley next to their co-op, the husband appeared to be more upset by her missing jewelry than by the bullet in her brain.

Kate and Charlie had ordered room service and gone to work. Based on the suspects' alibis and what they'd been doing during the days leading up to the murder, Charlie and Kate had figured out a timeline for each of them.

Both the attorney and the stepdaughter had eaten lunch at Serendipity's across the street from Bloomingdale's on the day of the murder. Two different homicide detectives had interviewed them and hadn't made the connection.

How well did the attorney know the step-daughter?

As it turned out, well enough to have convinced the stepmother to leave her own considerable estate directly to her stepdaughter, and then to have hired a hit man to murder his client.

Charlie had been made Detective First Grade when he broke what the *Post* had dubbed The Case of the Killer Rockette and the Crooked Attorney. Charlie always had referred to it as Serendipity.

With all the red herrings surfacing in Stella Sajak's and Nancy Cooper's murders, Kate desperately needed to review the timelines and motives for all the suspects.

She pictured three possible scenarios for Wyndam Oberon.

1. Oberon had hired Timmy as a hit man and was paying him up front on the pier. But Timmy would have been unreliable, even if capable of murder. And why would he have delivered that note to Stella, casting suspicion on himself?

2. Oberon had hired Timmy to deliver the note and had been paying him for completing the job, then later Oberon himself had met and murdered Stella

on the beach. But could Oberon have killed two women?

3. Oberon had acted as a middleman for the murderer, and had hired Timmy to deliver the note that set up Stella's meeting on the beach with Oberon's killer client. But who could that client be?

Kate, leaning toward the third scenario, considered the players.

Stanley Ferris? Could the police actually have the right man in custody and now, based on her detective work, decide that they had the wrong man? She reached into her shirt pocket and pulled out a Pepcid AC.

David Fry? Sea Breeze's CEO's unbridled greed and corruption, thwarted by Stella's well-organized resistance, added up to a strong motive. Then there had been that killer look.

Joe Sajak? Hadn't he quickly called Oberon for advice when he'd been frightened that the police might arrest him? And he could have arrived in Palmetto Beach well before Tuesday night, hired the lawyer to serve as his middleman, and set Stella's murder in motion.

"A penny for your thoughts, or in today's market, maybe I should make that a dollar?"

At the sound of Joe Sajak's smooth baritone, Ballou barked, and Kate dropped her pooper-scooper.

TWENTY-TWO

"Sorry. I didn't mean to startle you," Joe said, then bent and picked up the pooper-scooper, handing it to her like a bouquet.

Kate could only stare at him. A not very tall, slight, good-looking, mild-mannered man, wearing a dark suit, white shirt, and muted tie — obviously ready for his dead wife's visitation — who, however inadvertently, had terrified her.

When she didn't respond, he continued, "It's just that I've been deep in thought myself. Stella's and that newspaper woman's murders keep haunting me. And then you could have been killed, too, Kate. I can't get those images out of my mind. I took a walk to try and clear my head."

Images that he'd conjured up or images that he'd actually seen? God! Had Nancy Cooper's last word been Joe? Kate remained uncertain. Could a double murderer be sharing his feelings?

Kate backed away from him, and stumbled. Ballou barked, positioning himself between Kate and Joe. Then the Westie growled and went for Joe's shin. Kate pulled him off.

"I don't think your dog likes me." Joe

leaned in and grabbed her arm. "You're very pale, Kate. Are you okay?"

Still unable to find her voice, she nodded. At five forty-five, A1A was bathed in sunshine, the late-afternoon rush-hour traffic filled its north- and southbound lanes, and a jogger waved as he ran by. Get a grip, girl. Joe's not about to shoot you in broad daylight, in front of witnesses.

"Kate?"

"Yes," she said, sounding squeaky. "I felt a little queasy there for a moment, but I'm fine now." An oily taste coated her mouth, yet her lips were dry. She wondered if Joe knew that Oberon had been spotted with Timmy up in Del Ray Beach and that the police now had a witness who could connect the attorney to the newsboy. If Oberon had acted as Joe's middleman, Kate figured he'd have contacted his client immediately after that pay phone fiasco. A rush of anger swept away her fear and she wrenched her arm away from Joe's grip.

"Did you hear from Wyndam Oberon this afternoon?"

Joe took a step back from Kate and Ballou and shook his head. "No, I spoke to him early this morning, before I went to the funeral parlor with Marlene. However, I've been trying to reach him to go over the final arrangements for Stella's ashes." Joe's eyes welled up, but Kate had no sympathy. "Why do you ask?"

185

Kate shrugged. "Mary Frances and I saw Oberon up in Del Ray this afternoon, talking to Timmy, the missing newsboy — who then vanished once again. But both the Del Ray and the Palmetto Beach Police had a long chat with Oberon . . ."

"What!?"

Either Joe Sajak had trained as an actor or the man was genuinely shocked. The latter wouldn't prove his innocence; only that Oberon hadn't called him yet.

"Yes, looks like your old pal Wyndam Oberon may need to hire an attorney."

"Oberon's no pal of mine, Kate." Joe pulled a crisp white handkerchief out of his breast pocket and wiped his brow. His clothes were way too warm for a stroll in South Florida's relentless sunshine. "I'd never even laid eyes on the man until I arrived in Palmetto Beach."

"Is that right?" With Ballou in the lead, the trio turned around and started back to the condo.

"Yes." Joe slipped out of his jacket and folded it neatly over his left arm. He was walking on the outside, an old-fashioned courtesy that Kate seldom saw these days. "And Oberon hasn't been very helpful. I'm trying to find out who gave Stella that two-hundred-thousand-dollar cashier's check, but he keeps on pitty-patting around my questions. I think he knows more than he's saying about these murders."

186

Could Joe be telling the truth? Kate waited.

"Like the yearbook," Joe said. "I asked him about that and he got all flustered."

"What yearbook?" He'd lost her.

"Stella's high school yearbook. I found it next to her bed with a yellow sticky on it. Stella liked to write on yellow pads and she always used a green pen."

Where was he going with this?

"Sure enough, the number 'two hundred thousand' was scrawled right across that yellow sticky. In green ink. So I knew that Stella had put it there."

"Why would she have done that?" Puzzling over this new information, Kate frowned. "How could that cashier's check — or the amount that it had been made out for — have anything to do with Stella's high school yearbook?"

"Beats me. I thought that Wyndam might know. But he acted really weird, then totally clammed up when I mentioned that Stella had ripped a page out of her yearbook. You know, I figured that had to be tied in — somehow — to the money."

Kate started. "What page was missing?"

"The one with the photographs of the Science Department. English, Spanish, even Shop — all those teachers' photos were present and accounted for. But Stella had yanked out the Science page, leaving only a jagged edge behind. Strange." Joe Sajak wiped his brow again. He'd be wilted before he even arrived at the funeral parlor.

"You went to school with Stella, right? Think. What reason could she have for removing that particular page? Someone special's photograph? A favorite teacher? Who was in the Science Department during your senior year?"

Kate thought: And why now? If Stella had torn out the page around the time that she received the check, had she recently gotten back in touch with one of her teachers? He or she would be well over eighty.

Joe looked deep in thought. "Well, the only science teacher that I remember is Mr. Baum." Joe's baritone took on an edge that had to be every bit as jagged as what was left of the missing page. "Martin Baum. I'll never forget him. He committed suicide on our graduation day. So he couldn't have had anything to do with that two-hundred-thousand-dollar check, now could he?"

A spectre from Stella's past . . . just as she and Marlene had predicted. "How well did Stella know this Mr. Baum? Could there have been something going on between them?" Kate could hear the excitement in her voice.

"Nothing!" Joe's baritone dropped into a booming bass. "That man had been sleeping with one of his students — or at least that's what his suicide note said. The student never

188

came forward, but I assure you, it wasn't my Stella!"

Right. "Of course not." Kate responded in her most soothing voice, then switched gears. "Joe, speaking of notes, did you or the police ever find the one that Timmy had dropped off for Stella?"

"No. And they searched for it. I did, too. After all, the cops had missed the significance of the sticky. Didn't Stella leave the lobby right after Miss Mitford handed her the note? She could have tossed it anywhere."

Yes. And no one had a clue where Stella had gone after reading the note. "I just hoped that she'd kept it."

They turned into the driveway and Ballou strained at his leash, giving a delighted yelp as Marlene, dressed in her best black pants suit, came barreling out the front door.

"I've been looking all over for you two. Kate, I've left at least five messages. Where have you been all afternoon? You're not even dressed. You certainly don't plan on going to a wake looking like that, do you? And Joe, I've been knocking on your door forever. I thought you wanted to get to the visitation early, to arrange the pictures or the flowers or whatever." Marlene shouted, making no attempt to conceal her annoyance. "I never suspected that the two of you had gone off together."

"We didn't go off together." Kate stammered

189

like a schoolgirl. Marlene had rattled her. "I was walking Ballou and ran into Joe." Then, embarrassed and more than a little annoyed herself, Kate went on the offensive. "Talking about taking off without an explanation, why didn't you tell me that you'd gone to Ireland's Inn last night?"

TWENTY-THREE

Joe Sajak scurried off "to change my shirt," leaving Marlene and Kate in the lobby. The face-to-face that Kate had wanted. Or had thought she wanted.

Marlene was flushed even though central air-conditioning kept Ocean Vista's public areas at an almost chilly 68 degrees. Beads of sweat danced on her forehead and upper lip. "Kate," she said, her chin sagging and her voice breaking, "what can I say?"

Marlene's contrite body language softened Kate's resolve. Then, remembering how Marlene had mastered the art of an abject apology that explained nothing, Kate steeled herself, saying, "Well, you can start with why you didn't tell me that you'd gone out last night."

She and Marlene had established a "don't ask; don't tell" policy long before the U.S. Army. There were areas of Marlene's life that Kate had never visited and probably wouldn't want to visit. Her former sister-in-law's late-night expedition to Ireland's Inn wasn't one of those areas.

Staring at the statue of Aphrodite directly behind Kate's head, Marlene mumbled, "I

191

was ashamed to tell you."

"Ashamed to tell me what?" Kate tried to keep her voice neutral, while fighting off suspicion.

"That I couldn't be alone." Her mumble had become more like a moan. "That I craved male attention. That I wanted to dance. That I didn't care that Stella's body hadn't even been cremated. That I left the dirty dishes and drove to Ireland's Inn to have some fun. That I ran into Stanley Ferris and he asked me to dance and I realized that my behavior was every bit as sleazy as his. That I left right after he did, and came home, took a toddy to bed with me, and turned on AMC."

Somehow Marlene's words comforted Kate. Good Lord, what had she expected to hear? That Marlene had gone to the Gazette Building? It was Kate's turn to feel ashamed.

"Marlene . . ."

"And then, when you needed me, I wasn't there for you. You called me, but I was out dancing and you went over to Nancy's office" — a huge sob escaped, making Marlene gasp — "and someone tried to kill you. And it's all my fault."

"Marlene, it's not your fault —"

"And then this morning, I tried to sound happy when I called to tell you that the cops were hauling Stanley out of the hot tub." Marlene took a breath and paused, as if re-

192

flecting on what she'd just said. "Well, actually, I *was* happy about Stanley being carted off to jail, but down deep I knew that I'd failed you."

Kate chuckled. "Mary Frances and I felt happy about Stanley, too."

"And then you went off with the dancing nun and never left me a message. I guess I deserved that."

"You don't deserve anything but the best." Kate leaned over and kissed Marlene's cheek. "Why don't we just drop this conversation and get back to murder?"

Marlene seemed to relax. "Okay." A smile spread slowly across her face. "I still don't think Stanley's our killer. He told me at Ireland's Inn that he was heading over to Federal Highway to the Pink Pussycat, that's a lap dance joint, less than a block from the Palmetto Beach Gazette Building. I'll bet he parked in the Gazette's lot and decided to use their bathroom — it would be a far better choice than the Pink Pussycat's john, that's for sure."

Kate nodded. "Have you shared that theory with Detective Carbone?"

"No. I didn't want to admit that I'd been at Ireland's Inn."

"We'll tell him tonight. And after the visitation, I need you to help me create a timeline for Timmy. But first, let me tell you about Wyndam Oberon."

193

★ ★ ★

Though Kate had showered and dressed in record time, she kept Mary Frances waiting for almost fifteen minutes.

Now they couldn't find a spot in the Adams Family Mortuary's parking lot.

Mary Frances said, "I can't believe this, Kate. It's almost seven-thirty." She'd been checking her watch and complaining ever since they'd met in the lobby. "I pride myself on never being late for a wedding or a wake."

Kate sighed then, for the third time, said, "I'm sorry."

Marlene had no worries about Mary Frances replacing her as Kate's best friend. If Kate hadn't promised Nick Carbone that she wouldn't go anywhere alone, she would have taken her own car and avoided all this nagging. Maybe with Wyndam Oberon looking guilty, Carbone would ease his ban on Kate's solo travel. She wondered if the police had questioned the attorney. Or if they'd even found him?

Samuel Adams, dressed all in white and looking like a cross between a Good Humor man and Kate's dentist, stood in the foyer in front of the Hepplewhite desk, greeting the mourners in hushed tones, and pointing the way to Viewing Room B.

The size of the crowd surprised Kate. Her

194

least favorite uncle had judged the worth of a man's life by the number of people who attended his wake. By Uncle Harry's standards, Stella Sajak's life had been a success.

Making her way through the crowd, she nodded at her neighbors and waved at Herb Wagner. Somewhere, off to the side, a harpist was playing Chopin. Marlene had told her there would be a table next to the urn where she could put her sympathy card.

Miss Mitford, wearing Victorian mourning garb, complete with an ecru eyelet collar, black stockings, and oxfords, sat in the front row, sandwiched between Jeanette Nelson and Mildred Green, dressed to disco. As Kate passed by the trio, she overheard Mildred telling Miss Mitford, "I never wear lavender." She kept moving.

"Psst. Hello there, Kate." She recognized Jeanette's lilt and turned around.

"We're going dancing at the Senior Center later, do you want to come along?"

"Sorry, Jeanette," Kate said, "not tonight. Can I have a rain check?"

"Where's Stella?" Mildred asked, though she was sitting close enough to the Persian urn to reach over and touch it. "I always like to check out the makeup. The Adams Family Mortuary's cosmetician tends to pile on the rouge and always uses the most unflattering mauve eye shadow. Makes her clients look sick. I don't see the casket. Have they stuck

Stella in another room?"

While Kate debated how to handle Mildred's question, and neither Mary Frances nor Jeanette uttered a word, Miss Mitford pointed to the urn.

Mildred shrugged. "In a bowl, is she? Well, at least, it isn't lavender."

Joe Sajak sat next to the urn, flanked by enormous baskets of lilies, talking to a tall, lanky Texan whom Kate recognized as an Ocean Vista board member. With the condo president dead and the vice-president in jail, would this cowboy become a candidate for president? Or would Joe run, jumping in — like the widows of U.S. Senators often do — to serve out his wife's term? Making a decision to attend the next board meeting, she could hear Charlie chuckle.

As the Texan moved on, Joe stood and fussed over the photographs of Stella on the large marble top table next to the urn. Several of her personal things were on display as well: a royal blue silk scarf, a mother-of-pearl box, and a ruby slipper, not unlike Dorothy's. And off to one side, her yearbook.

Kate fought the temptation to snatch it up, search out a quiet corner, and go through it page by page. As if Charlie had whispered in her ear, she suddenly felt convinced that the motive for Stella's murder had sprung from her past, and that the yearbook contained a clue to her killer. She had to get her hands on it. Tonight. Before someone else . . .

"Good evening, Mrs. Kennedy. Are you all right?" David Fry sounded solicitous, yet patronizing. "You look as if you've seen a ghost."

"Well, this would be the place to see one, wouldn't it, Mr. Fry? And there's nothing like a good ghost story, is there?" As he opened his mouth to reply, Kate walked away.

The huge crowd, tough to navigate through, reminded her of Stella's last stand at Town Hall — and her own nagging senior moment. "Damn."

Only as Marlene giggled did Kate realize that she'd spoken aloud.

She turned around to find Marlene accompanied by an intense young man with tousled hair, horn-rim glasses, and wearing a tweed jacket.

The young man smiled. "I know. I know. The fabric's a fashion faux pas for fall in South Florida, but it's the only jacket I own." He had a New York accent, probably Queens, and a sincere, if nasal, delivery. She liked him instantly.

"Kate Kennedy, this is Jeff Stein, the editor of the *Palmetto Beach Gazette*," Marlene said, "and we've been chatting about Nancy Cooper."

"Nice to meet you, Mrs. Kennedy. I'm really sorry about what happened to you the other night when you tried to save Nancy."

A pang of guilt took Kate by surprise. She'd been so focused on Stella's murder that she'd hardly thought about Nancy's.

"I'm so sorry that I arrived too late. I didn't know Nancy Cooper well, but she seemed to love her work at the paper."

"A good reporter," Jeff said. "We'll miss her."

"Will she be buried in Palmetto Beach?" Kate didn't know if she could face another funeral.

"No. The coroner promised to release Nancy's body by tomorrow afternoon. Her sister will fly here and bring her back to Iowa." Owl-like, Jeff peered over his glasses. "And he also confirmed that the same caliber gun killed both victims."

Kate could still feel that gun at her head — so real — that she wondered who was behind her. She spun around to check, her eyes sweeping the room. The widower seemed absorbed in animated conversation with the mayor and two of her councilmen. Mary Frances and the tall Texan were chatting like old friends. Jeanette and Mildred were saying good-bye to Samuel Adams. Miss Mitford was riffling through the sympathy cards. But no one was standing anywhere near Kate.

"Are you okay?" Kate knew that Marlene's query had been prompted by genuine concern, but she worried that her emotions could be so easily read.

"Yes. Sorry. I just had a bad moment, but it passed." Kate smiled. "I'm fine now."

Theories tumbled through her head. She didn't want the editor to leave until she asked him a couple of questions. Jeff Stein had kind eyes and an eager-to-please manner. She was about to test those qualities.

"Nancy Cooper had three stories ready to roll in Thursday's *Gazette*." Kate tried to sound firm, but fair. "Stella's obit. An exposé on David Fry. And a mysterious hot scoop. Yet you only published the obituary. What happened to the other two?"

Jeff laughed. "You're a gutsy lady. If you ever want a job as a reporter, Mrs. Kennedy, give me a call."

"A good reporter's questions get answered." Kate held his gaze.

"Okay. The mystery scoop remains just that. I knew Nancy was chasing after another big story, but I never saw it." Jeff Stein sighed. "And her David Fry exposé didn't have two sources, so I couldn't print it. Not then, anyway."

"What do you mean, not then?" Anticipation coated Kate's words.

"I'm printing an Extra tonight — a special edition — we've never done that before." He looked smug. Like her son Kevin had when he received an unexpected A in Trig.

"About David Fry?" Marlene asked.

"Yes. Of course, he'll deny everything, but the Broward County State's Attorney has launched an investigation into David Fry's Sea Breeze Corporation. The alleged charges include bribery, fraud, and cooking the books." Jeff Stein grinned. "And do you know why the third councilman isn't here tonight?"

Kate and Marlene just stared at the editor.

"Because he's not as brazen as David Fry, but Councilman Jerome Clark is also under investigation, alleged to have accepted a bribe from Sea Breeze. He could end up as Fry's cell mate."

TWENTY-FOUR

"Hello!" A loud, raspy, all-too-familiar voice filled the room. "I just drew the 'get out of jail free' card." Kate jerked her head around toward the double doors. Stanley Ferris had arrived at Stella Sajak's wake.

A brief stunned silence was quickly followed by nervous chatter as Stella's mourners tried not to stare at the man who'd been arrested for her murder.

Stanley posed in the doorway — there was no other way to describe that stance — hands on hips, pelvis thrust forward, like an aging rock star greeting his fans. Last seen in handcuffs and a skimpy bathing suit, Stanley now wore a cream-colored blazer, black silk pants, and his signature alligator cowboy boots. Obviously, he'd gone home to change before making his entrance.

"Damn." Jeff Stein sounded pained. "His timing sucks. The presses are rolling. An hour earlier, I could have interviewed him for the Extra."

Kate felt torn, wanting to hear more about David Fry and the crooked councilman — Jeff Stein was a font of information — and wanting to know how Stanley

Ferris had gotten out of jail.

Where was Nick Carbone? Had Oberon been arrested? Could the attorney actually have pulled the trigger? Or had he hired Timmy to do more than deliver a note? Had Oberon confessed?

Maybe the last word that Nancy had uttered hadn't been *Joe*. Or *yo*. Or even *oh*. Maybe what she'd heard Nancy say was *O* as in Oberon. Kate's stomach churned: That made sense. Wyndam Oberon, the unlikeliest murderer since the two little old ladies in *Arsenic and Old Lace*, had killed Stella and Nancy, and then held a smoking gun to her head.

But why? What was his motive? Had Oberon been part of Stella's life before Palmetto Beach? Kate's eyes moved from the doorway to the table that held the yearbook. How old was he anyway? Could he have been in high school with Stella and Joe? The attorney might be about the right age, but he couldn't have grown up in suburban Michigan, not with that syrupy, Southern drawl. Maybe, despite Charlie's *message*, the motive hadn't been rooted in Stella's mysterious past, but in her combative present. Unless . . .

"Kate." Marlene startled her. "Jeff is leaving." Marlene's emphasis on "leaving" signaled that if Kate had any more questions, she'd better ask them now.

"I'll get up early tomorrow morning to

read your Extra," Kate said, extending her hand to Jeff Stein. "One more question, if I may."

"Shoot."

"Do you have any idea what Nancy Cooper's third story might have been about? Even a hint. I think she was murdered to kill that story."

A glint of admiration appeared in Jeff's brown eyes. "You are dogged, Mrs. K. And I meant what I said earlier. If you ever want a job as a reporter, give me a call." He reached into his pocket and handed Kate a card. "I have no clue what Nancy's third story was about, but I'll ask the police to check her computer files, and who knows, maybe they might even come across a disk — if they can find anything in all that clutter."

"Thank you," Kate said, "but I'd bet that the killer erased the file and took the disk."

With a little nod, Jeff disappeared into the crowd.

"Look at the sappy expression on Joe Sajak's face." Marlene almost growled. "He's smitten with the mayor."

Once again, Kate turned away from the entrance where Stanley, like a conquering hero, was greeting his well-wishers with smiles and pats on the back.

Joe and Brenda Walters, engrossed in animated conversation, did appear to have eyes only for each other.

"When the widower spotted the mayor this afternoon at the Dew Drop Inn — immediately after watching his wife's cremation, I might add — he seemed transfixed and told me that she reminded him of a movie star." Marlene shook her head. "Then he proceeded to down a bacon cheeseburger with four thousand French fries — no doubt smothering his grief in grease."

"You think it's all an act, don't you?"

"Yes. No. I don't know." Marlene laughed. A roar deep from the gut, reminding Kate of the happy laughter they'd shared as children. "Do you?"

"At the very least, I think he's overacting, trying to prove how much he cared. But I don't know why."

"To cover up a motive for murder?"

Fascinated, Kate watched as Joe whispered something in the mayor's ear. Brenda Walters smiled and touched his forearm.

"Now isn't that cozy?" Marlene said. "Come on, let's go over and join them."

As Kate and Marlene approached Brenda Walters and Joe Sajak from the left, David Fry barreled in from the right, and Stanley, making his way from the double doors, swept down the center. Feeling childish, Kate picked up speed.

Fry got there first.

Kate could hear the mayor telling him, "No. I will not schedule a special meeting.

Jerome Clark has, at my request, and with the approval of the other two members, been temporally removed from the council, pending the outcome of the State's Attorney's investigation. As of now, it doesn't look good for your buddy, Clark."

"I think you're overreacting, Mayor Walters." Fry sounded considerably less charming than usual.

"And I can't believe that you've put my administration in this position, Mr. Fry."

Kate wondered if their formal manner of address was for the benefit of their growing audience.

Stanley Ferris squeezed in between the mayor and the widower, and spoke to Joe. "Let an innocent man offer his sincere condolences." He held out his hand.

Joe backed away from him, almost knocking over the urn. He caught it; then cupped his right hand over the lid as if to protect Stella's remains.

"Would a guilty man show up at his victim's funeral?"

Obviously, Stanley had never read any of Agatha Christie's cozies.

The dentist was now almost nose to nose with Joe. "Stella was my colleague on the Ocean Vista Board of Directors. And I respected her."

"Stanley," Marlene said, "there isn't a woman dead or alive that you ever respected."

205

"Marlene Friedman, you have a big mouth," Stanley shrieked.

Samuel Adams popped out from the wall of burgundy drapes behind the urn and announced, "Visitation hours are over."

TWENTY-FIVE

The pizzas arrived at 9:45 p.m. One plain — out of deference to Kate's digestive system — the other topped with sausage, peppers, and onions. Mary Frances, Marlene, and Kate had accepted Joe Sajak's invitation to stop by his place and order in — he'd added that he didn't want to be alone.

Though Kate was ravenous — lunch at Del Ray had been hours ago — she'd wanted to get back to her own apartment and work on Timmy's timeline. Stella's too. Spotting the yearbook in Joe's hand as they left the funeral parlor, she'd said, "Count me in."

The yearbook was now on the breakfront, inches away from the Persian urn. Odd. Joe had let Marlene carry Stella's ashes, but he'd carried the yearbook.

Just as she and Mary Frances had berated Stanley all the way home, his bad behavior continued to be the prime topic of conversation.

"Why in the world did the police let him go?" Joe had asked this question twice before.

This time Marlene fielded it. "Because your attorney, Wyndam Oberon, is looking and acting mighty guilty. And because Nick Carbone never really believed that Stanley

Ferris was a killer. It's snowbird season and the mayor and council wanted the case closed." Marlene flipped a slice of pizza on a paper plate and passed it to Kate. "You know, Joe, the way the mayor was pushing the chief of police to make an arrest, you should consider yourself lucky that you weren't the scapegoat."

Kate devoured her slice, washed it down with Diet Coke, and reached for another.

"The mayor is an interesting woman and most attractive . . . and she seems so familiar . . . like a television anchor," Joe said as he turned toward the pizza box.

Over his bent head, Marlene winked at Kate. "I thought she looked like a movie star."

"I gather that the mayor and Stella had some differences," Joe said, ignoring Marlene's comment, "but she seems to be genuinely distraught . . ."

"You might want to remember that she's a politician," Mary Frances said.

Kate wiped her hands with a paper napkin. "May I look at Stella's yearbook?"

"Well, I — er — I . . ." Joe stammered.

Kate felt herself flush. Why didn't he want her to see the yearbook?

Joe put down his pizza. "I guess that would be okay, but I'd like you to wash your hands before you touch it."

"No problem." She stood. "Is the bathroom down the hall?"

Marlene held a hand over her mouth. Kate suspected she was stifling laughter.

"Yes, next to the guest room. Please don't use the ecru towel with the white embroidery. That's Stella's handiwork and I consider it an heirloom."

"Okay," Kate said. "And why don't you fill in Marlene and Mary Frances on the missing page."

The guest bathroom was charming — brass sconces, an old-fashioned pedestal sink, white wood planking on the floor — and immaculate. Had Stella been this tidy and clean? Or had her anal retentive widower given it a scrub-down? Kate washed her hands, wiped off the soap dish, and used a plain white terry hand towel.

On her way back, she popped into the guest bedroom. Again, very grandmother's cottage in decor. Joe's suitcases were neatly stacked in one corner. She opened the closet. His jackets, shirts, and pants were hanging there, two inches between each garment; shoes lined up like soldiers. So Joe wasn't sleeping in the master bedroom. Because of his grief? Because he didn't want to mess it up? Or because he and Stella hadn't been sharing a bed during their *Same Time, Next Year* reunions?

"Can I help you with something?" Joe took her by surprise.

Staring at the hook rug on the highly polished wood floor, she said, "Er, sorry, just nosy, I guess. It's so pretty."

She followed him back to the living room, feeling like a kid who'd been caught by the principal.

As the other three continued eating, Kate picked up the yearbook, treating it as if it were a first edition, and sat in an armchair far removed from the food.

She turned to the jagged edge of the missing page. "By any chance would there be another picture of the science teacher?"

"Yes," Joe said, "in the back. Under Science Club. There's a picture of Martin Baum with Stella and some of his other honor students."

Kate flipped to the back and found the photo. Martin Baum, a horse-faced man in his mid-thirties, with thinning fair hair and thick glasses, was surrounded by three girls and one boy. Rather uncharitably, Kate decided that not one of them, including the teacher, could be called even remotely attractive. All five were focused on a Bunsen burner. One of the girls held a clipboard. The boy held a vial.

Joe, Mary Frances, and Marlene came over and circled Kate's chair.

Kate pointed to the girl in the center, who sported a mane of fuzzy dark curls. "Is this Stella?"

"That's my sweetheart."

The girl to Stella's right had stringy brown hair, which looked in need of a good wash, and a bumpy nose. The other girl was overweight, with acne. The boy looked like a younger version of Martin Baum.

"Who are these other kids?" Kate asked. "Can you tell me something about them? They're only identified as honor students."

Joe walked around and stood next to Kate. "God, let me think. The guy is Howie Gordon. He was in my homeroom. A real bookworm. The heavyset girl is Sophie Stefanos. Or some name like that. Her father owned a diner. The family had some money. Most of us were working-class poor. And I think the other girl is Bea Wernoski. Lived in a trailer. Her mother was a widow. Dirt poor, but smart. They were all smart. Howie won a scholarship to Princeton. Why do you want to know all this?"

Kate shrugged. "The science teacher committed suicide. He was rumored to be having an affair with one of his students. I wanted to see what he looked like. And I wanted to know something about Stella's classmates. No real reason. Just curious."

"Yes, I noticed your curiosity in the guest bedroom." Joe lifted the yearbook off Kate's lap.

"Whoa," Marlene said, "you didn't wash your hands!"

TWENTY-SIX

Seated at the kitchen table, armed with mugs of decaf Lipton — she and Marlene had to get some sleep tonight — and two huge pieces of Entenmann's yellow cake with chocolate icing, their long-standing favorite, Kate finally was getting to work on the timelines.

Ballou snuggled in Marlene's lap, loving the attention and the bits of cake that she was feeding him.

"Okay, Ballou, your Aunt Marlene and I have work to do." Marlene put the Westie down and he stretched out between their chairs.

Kate handed Marlene a yellow pad, then held out a box of ballpoint pens and, doing a fair imitation of Joe Sajak's smooth baritone, asked, "Would you like a green pen, like Stella always used?"

"Sure. Maybe her spirit will inspire us."

Kate took a sip of tea. "I think we should start in the lobby on Tuesday afternoon. Timmy delivered the note while we were all at Town Hall and, for some reason, went back to work. You bought a newspaper from him on our way home from the meeting. Maybe he was just killing time until his appointment with Oberon. Hmm — I wonder how Timmy felt when he saw Stella in the car with us. Anyway, we arrived in the lobby around three-thirty, and Miss Mitford handed Stella the note. I remember being impressed with the quality of the paper."

"Good taste eliminates Stanley, right?"

"Probably."

"Should I make columns?" Marlene sounded wide awake and ready to roll at 11 p.m. on what felt like the longest day of Kate's life. "I can put each suspect's name at the top of a column, do the timeline along the margin, and then, under each name, enter where that suspect was — or wasn't — at any given time."

"Sounds like a plan." Kate smiled. "I'm glad Mary Frances decided to go straight to bed. You know, she'd offered to help with the timelines, but I'd rather work with you."

The glow on Marlene's face flooded Kate with warm memories. As little kids, she and Marlene played with movie star paper dolls, creating their own scenarios for Lana Turner and Betty Grable that, sometimes, seemed better than the stars' Hollywood plots.

And later, as gawky twelve-year-olds, they wrote and starred in their own plays, assigning the supporting roles to their less ambitious friends. They'd performed on a makeshift stage in Kate's basement, dressed up in her mother's flapper gowns. And Kate's mother in an apron, far removed from her dancing days in the Roaring Twenties, would serve hot chocolate and crumb buns fresh from the German bakery around the corner and would applaud their performances, shouting, "Author, author."

Marlene held up her artwork. "Ready. You talk; I'll enter."

"Okay. David Fry, Stanley, Mary Frances, Stella, you, and I were at Town Hall with the mayor when the note was delivered. Joe Sajak claims that he was down in Fort Lauderdale at Pier 66 on his friend's sailboat, but like his alibi for the time of the murder, that can't be confirmed. We don't know where Wyndam Oberon was, but we do know that at a little after four, he was seen talking to Timmy on the pier. Timmy had a martini at the Neptune Inn right after their conversation, then disappeared. Maybe the attorney had advised him to get out of town. Did Oberon murder Stella and Nancy?" Kate shrugged. "His actions today certainly indicate that he's our killer, but I believe he was a middleman. God, when he gave Timmy that note, he may not even have known he was aiding and abetting a murderer."

"Where did Stella go when she left the lobby?" Marlene filled in the timelines as she spoke. "She dashed right out the front door after she'd read the note. Do you think that someone picked her up?"

"Where did Stella go? That's the sixty-four-dollar question. And why didn't we ask it earlier?"

Marlene screwed up her face in the chipmunk-like expression of bewilderment that she'd used ever since they were kids. "Even if I'd thought of the question, I wouldn't have had a clue as to the answer." She shook her head. "I still don't."

"What if that note scared the hell out of Stella? What if she had been blackmailing someone? And what if that note was an invitation — or a demand — to meet that someone — who'd already given her a two-hundred-thousand-dollar cashier's check — on the beach? And what if Stella had left the lobby, gone to the parking lot, got into her own car, and driven over to the Gazette Building to give Nancy Cooper a heads-up, so that if something happened to her, Nancy would have the dirt on her murderer? And what if after Stella's death, Nancy called the person Stella had been blackmailing to ask some questions and the killer realized that Nancy knew the truth and shot her, too."

"Those are a lot of *what-ifs*, Kate. You remind me of when we were kids, playing movie stars and plotting those plays."

"But this plot is for real. Nancy had to die . . ."

"To kill the third story. Nancy's big scoop that Jeff Stein never saw."

Kate nodded. "Exactly."

"David Fry," Marlene said. "Nancy Cooper spent a lot of time with him following Stella's murder and went to great lengths to convince us that she and he were good friends, and maybe more. Could there have been yet another skeleton in his closet in addition to the corruption, fraud, and bribery story that's supposed to run tonight? What else could Fry be guilty of? Maybe a major personal scandal. Something kinky? Like an orgy with the mayor and her three councilmen?"

Kate drained her tea. "Or maybe a secret from his and Stella's and Joe Sajak's past. I wonder where David Fry grew up."

Marlene had slipped Ballou another morsel of cake and he was still licking her fingers long after the last of the icing was gone. Kate felt a pang of jealousy. Would Charlie's dog always prefer Marlene?

"That's why you were checking out the yearbook!" Marlene pounded the table. Ballou jumped up, ready for action and looked dejected when ignored. "And our host wasn't happy about your snooping. If Stella was killed because of something that happened almost a half-century ago, I think Joe Sajak must be our man."

"Me, too." Kate pushed her hair off her face. "I guess." She couldn't recall ever having been this tired. "Except . . ."

"What?"

"I'm not sure . . . but I'd like to get another look at that yearbook."

"Listen, you've had a rough few days, Kate. Go to bed. At eight-thirty tomorrow morning, I'm helping Samuel Adams turn Ocean Vista's rec room into 'a nonreligious yet chapel-like sanctuary, with her urn surrounded by flowers. A farewell scene suited to Stella's personality.' Personality doesn't come cheap. I think the flowers alone are over a thousand dollars."

Kate managed a weak laugh.

"So get some rest." Marlene put the yellow pad on the table. "We can finish these timelines after the memorial. And I promise, even if I have to steal it, you'll get to read Stella's yearbook."

Kate had stacked the dishwasher and was wiping off the table when the phone rang. Ballou yelped and Kate said, "Quiet." Then, feeling guilty, she petted his head.

"Hello?" Who would be calling her this late? Could one of her kids . . .

"Nick Carbone, Kate."

"Oh. Hi. What's wrong?"

He chuckled. "Yeah, I guess I never call with good news, do I?"

"Well . . ." She felt like yelping herself.

"We found Wyndam Oberon. He didn't answer the door. His place was locked up like Fort Knox. And it took forever for the judge to issue a search warrant, so I've just left his house."

"What did he say?" Her hand clenched.

"He's dead, Kate. We found him fully dressed, sitting at his desk in the bedroom. He'd been shot in the head with what we think is the murder weapon. We couldn't find a note, but the ME says it looks like suicide."

"And what do you say? Do you believe he killed himself?"

"Well, we haven't found Timmy and I hate loose ends, but yes, I think it's suicide."

"So the killer's dead. Can I go out alone now and not worry?"

Carbone sighed. "Until the autopsy is completed and I review the final report on the weapon, watch your back, Kate."

She hung up sad and shaken, and wondering how Stella's science teacher had committed suicide.

TWENTY-SEVEN

Still in her terry cloth robe and bedroom slippers, Kate carried her and Ballou's breakfast out to the balcony. Surprisingly, she'd slept well, her exhausted body shutting down her troubled mind for eight blessed hours.

Another designer day. Somehow, this morning, she didn't resent the "as promised by the Chamber of Commerce" weather. The sun was still high enough in the heavens to let the breeze from the aquamarine ocean work its magic, and the baby blue sky was almost cloudless. A perfect day for a wedding. Or a funeral. Stella, the beach lover, would have approved.

The *Palmetto Beach Gazette* Extra had arrived at her front door sometime during the night. She spread strawberry jam on her bagel, sipped her tea, put on her glasses, and read the headline:

CAN DAVID FRY TAKE THE HEAT?

And the lead:

ICE RINK BURNS BROWARD COUNTY STATE'S ATTORNEY.

Jeff Stein had a sense of humor. Could he have been serious about offering her a job? She read on with glee:

Councilman Jerome Clark held secret negotiations with David Fry, CEO of Sea Breeze Inc., in January of this year. These negotiations resulted in Clark receiving $500,000 and the promise of a Vice-President's position in the Sea Breeze Corporation, in exchange for presenting to the council the corporation's plans to raze the Palmetto Beach waterfront and construct a multimillion-dollar hotel complex and ice rink in its place, and convincing the mayor and his fellow councilmen to award the project to David Fry's Sea Breeze Inc.

Sources close to Fry say this was the same method he'd employed to obtain a similar contract for a multiplex Sports Arena in Coconut Cove. Those same sources are now cooperating fully with the Broward County State's Attorney's Office. With former Coconut Cove mayor Frank Larkin currently serving as Sea Breeze's Vice-President of Public Relations, under an ongoing investigation, yesterday afternoon Coconut Cove's councilman Barry Oskar resigned. Requesting anonymity, another council member alleged that Oskar had made a deal and would testify as a witness for the prosecution when the Broward County State's Attorney convenes a Grand Jury.

So golden boy David Fry was tarnished.

A flush of pleasure started at her toes and ended in a smile. Like Charlie, Kate believed the bad guys should be punished. It looked like Stella Sajak might win a posthumous victory. If so, the pier and the waterfront would remain intact and David Fry wouldn't be razing Ocean Vista to build a parking garage.

Kate raised her teacup toward the sky. "Good going, Stella!"

Kate and Ballou hit the beach at eight-thirty. Following his lead, she turned north toward the pier. Except for a jogger and another dog walker, she had the beach to herself. And Ocean Vista's chaises were empty, too.

As they passed the pool area, Kate watched all the activity going on near the glass doors that led into the recreation room. Two men, dressed in white cutaways, were carrying tall baskets filled with white roses. No wonder Stella's flower bill had been so bloody expensive. And from a van, parked on the north side of the building, two more men were unloading white satin slipcovers. Joan Crawford came to mind. No bare metal chairs allowed at a memorial service directed by the Adams Family Mortuary.

On this glorious morning, Kate didn't want to deal with death and she'd deliberately ignored Nick Carbone's advice about not going out alone. "Come on, Ballou, let's walk along the surf."

As a gentle wave rolled over her foot and a seagull soared above her head, she felt close to Charlie, almost as if she could reach out and touch him.

"You'll never walk alone . . ."

Kate almost tripped over Ballou. Could that sweet soprano be an angel singing? Had she lost her mind?

A lovely girl about her granddaughter Katharine's age and her Pekinese passed by on Kate's left. "Sorry, I didn't mean to startle you. Sometimes, I don't realize how far my voice carries." The girl and her dog had the same tawny color hair.

"Not at all. You sing beautifully." Kate smiled. "And that's one of my favorite songs."

Ballou sniffed the trembling Pekinese from stem to stern, then seemed to lose interest.

"Hi. I'm Kate Kennedy and that sniffer over there is Ballou."

"Nice to meet you. I'm Jennifer Holland," the girl said, then pointed to her dog, "and this is Serendipity."

"Serendipity?"

"Yes." Jennifer laughed. "She used to be Samantha, but that's so passé, don't you

222

think? So I changed her name and now she's Serendipity."

Kate felt her heart leap. Of course. Serendipity. A message from Charlie. He's sent the clue that could crack this case.

She needed more color in her cheeks. Kate wanted to look as good and as strong as possible today. And black could drain the color from your face.

Charlie used to say that perception and image were sometimes all a detective had going for him. Or her. Kate's challenge today would be to prove her theory — no easy task. She couldn't wait to get her hands on Stella's yearbook.

After taking a half hour to apply her makeup, she revisited her hair and put a few rollers on top. A little height wouldn't hurt. She hadn't fussed like this since Charlie died. It felt right; she wanted him to be proud of her.

The black silk pants suit was slimming. She added her mother's pearls, a single, matinee-length strand, and matching earrings, and stepped into her black leather pumps. Then she switched the essentials — keys, cash, and comb — from her camel tote bag to her small black purse. Pausing in front of the full-length mirror, she thought: Not bad for an old gal heading to a funeral. She could swear that she heard Charlie agree.

The service started at ten. She checked her watch: nine forty-five. She decided to go down to the lobby and get her mail. During that very long yesterday, she'd forgotten to pick it up.

Miss Mitford manned her station, though she'd dressed in her mourning attire and looked grim.

"Good morning, Miss Mitford," Kate said. "Are you going to Stella Sajak's memorial?"

"Yes. I'm closing up shop in five minutes. And the desk will stay closed out of respect for Mrs. Sajak for the rest of the weekend. So those who haven't collected their mail or messages will just have to wait till Monday." She sniffed. Inconveniencing the condo owners seemed to please her. "Would you like your mail now?"

"Yes, thank you." Kate fought an impulse to curtsy. The woman reminded her of Sister Leonarda, her high school principal, who'd instilled fear in the souls of her charges.

"Here, Mrs. Kennedy, take one of these flyers, too." Miss Mitford handed Kate an eight-by-ten sheet of white paper, bordered in black. Its bold words were in black, too.

During these sad times, with Stella Sajak's demise, please remember that Ocean Vista's Board of Directors needs a smooth transition of government.

In our upcoming special election, vote for Stanley Ferris, DDS, your current Vice-President, to serve as your new President.

Experience Counts!

The Stanley Ferris Election Committee

Rage swept through Kate like a hurricane. No way would that man be elected president. She'd make sure of that. And revenge, not rage, would be her weapon.

TWENTY-EIGHT

"What do you mean you can't write a check, Mrs. Friedman? You're the executrix, aren't you?" Samuel Adams puffed out his chest as he directed one of the catering staff to the recreation room's kitchen.

Marlene was going crazy. Since all the waiters were wearing white, she couldn't tell them apart from the undertakers. And both groups were scurrying around like an invasion of Palmetto bugs.

"The Adams Family Mortuary doesn't press to be paid immediately for services rendered." What a pompous jerk Samuel Adams was. "But the Carlyle Caterers aren't as accommodating."

A large, unsmiling, square-jawed woman holding a tray of quiches said, "Damn straight," then looked at the funeral director and laughed.

"Lower your voice, Mrs. Carlyle," Adams snapped. "The mourners are being seated."

"Well, if you want those mourners fed and watered, you better get me a check, pronto."

Marlene had to admit the recreation room looked lovely and she gave Samuel Adams all — well, most of the credit. With the drapes wide open, the Atlantic Ocean was aquamarine, highlighted with whitecaps, and the sun's golden rays became the backdrop for Stella's urn. The white slipcovers made the metal chairs look warm and inviting. And the dozen tall baskets, filled with white roses, were an elegant — if expensive — touch.

Adams had brought along an Edwardian era console table to hold the urn, the old photographs, and the yearbook. Joe Sajak was fussing around with those mementos. Sympathy cards were displayed, and could be dropped off, on a round table positioned near the door that led to the lobby. A man in white stood behind that table. Though she couldn't be certain, she thought he was part of the funeral, not the wait, staff.

Mrs. Carlyle pointed to Joe Sajak. "That's the widower, right?"

Marlene nodded.

"Okay hold this." The caterer shoved the tray at Marlene. "I'll get a check from him."

And she did.

Joe stopped rearranging Stella's relics, dashed upstairs, and returned with a check. As he passed Marlene, who'd put the quiche in the kitchen, he said, "When the estate is settled, I expect to be reimbursed."

It was the kind of morning that even as it unfolded seemed blurred. A morning of memories destined to be hazy. Faces lost in the crowd. Garbled words of grief.

Maybe that was how family and friends

made it through a funeral.

The pianist, a painfully thin young man whom Samuel Adams employed at all of his nonsectarian funerals — churches and synagogues usually having their own organists — played the opening bars of "Nearer My God to Thee." The memorial service had started.

Marlene took a seat in the second row, behind Joe Sajak, and waved Kate and Mary Frances over to join her. Mary Frances said, "The *Titanic*'s theme song. Why would Stella have requested that? I thought she didn't believe in God."

Joe spun around and gave Mary Frances a dirty look.

Marlene whispered to Kate, "So where's Wyndam Oberon? This has turned into a real mess. There are bills to be paid. Someone needs to settle Stella's estate."

Kate whispered back, "Dead."

Joe Stein, in the row behind them, said, "Suicide. Right. If you buy that, I'll sell you an acre in the Everglades."

The music stopped and Samuel Adams stood at the microphone directly to the left of the urn. The mourners sat at attention as he gave a dramatic reading of the Twenty-Third Psalm. Stella Sajak may have lived as an atheist, but the funeral director — or maybe the widower — had decided to give her a true believer's send-off.

When the reading was over, the pianist

played and sang a selection of Cole Porter songs, including "Miss Otis Regrets."

Then Joe Sajak stood, walked over to his wife's urn, placed both hands on it, and from memory, recited Elizabeth Barrett Browning's most beloved sonnet. Before he even got to, *"Let me count the ways,"* Marlene, Kate, and Mary Frances were all in tears.

Breaking the silence that followed Sajak's performance, Jeff Stein poked his head between Marlene and Kate and whispered, "The State's Attorney's Office carted off Nancy Cooper's computer this morning."

Back at the microphone, Samuel Adams, a better memorial master of ceremonies than Marlene had imagined, asked if any of the mourners wanted to say a few words about the deceased.

With so many of Stella's neighbors in attendance, most of the eulogies were pretty much the same until Stanley Ferris took the mike. "You all know that I discovered Stella's body and was, unjustly, arrested for her murder. Now I want to continue her fight to save Ocean Vista."

Marlene watched Kate's jaw clench and was about to speak when a crisp clear voice announced from the back of the room, "I'd like to say a few words, please."

Mayor Brenda Walters was down the aisle and at the mike before Stanley seemed to realize that he'd been upstaged.

Wearing a navy blue suit and white blouse, accessorized with expensive navy leather pumps and tote bag, the mayor looked as crisp as she sounded. She smiled warmly at her audience. "Stella Sajak proved to be not only a community activist, but a worthy opponent. I will miss her feisty spirit. But I want you all to know that Stella's spirit will live on. She fought the good fight and now she has won the battle to save Ocean Vista and Palmetto Beach's waterfront and pier. Recent events have proven that Stella Sajak was right about the questionable business practices of the Sea Breeze Corporation and that my council and I had been duped." The mayor rolled her eyes toward the ceiling and clasped her hands as if in prayer. "You have my word: There will be no rink, no razing, and no restoration, during my reign as mayor."

The Ocean Vista residents gave the mayor a standing ovation.

Marlene said, "We just witnessed a miracle here. Our mayor morphed from Machiavelli to Mother Teresa."

Then as the pianist's rousing rendition of "The Music of the Night" filled the room, she, Kate, and Mary Frances followed Joe, carrying the urn, out toward the pool area.

On the beach, a tall, overtanned man wearing jeans, a baseball cap, and sunglasses stood under a palm tree. When

Marlene looked his way, he waved.

Holy God! She gasped, stumbled, and almost fell into the pool.

The man was Timmy.

TWENTY-NINE

In the blazing midday sun, Kate watched as Marlene staggered, almost tumbling into the pool, then ran over to talk to some strange man on the beach. Kate squinted. He seemed vaguely familiar. Putting on her prescription sunglasses, she took a closer look. Timmy! He'd cleaned up some, and had on new clothes, and the baseball cap covered most of his sun-bleached hair, but that was Timmy.

Ugly, unconnected theories whirled through her mind and vied for her attention. Timmy and Marlene were standing under a palm tree, their heads together. Marlene doing most of the talking. Kate felt sick. Why *had* the newsboy called Marlene from Del Ray Beach? And why had he shown up this morning at Stella's memorial?

Kate glanced around, expecting to find all eyes on the odd couple. But no one else seemed to have noticed them. While the mourners waited for the reception to start, Joe, embracing Stella's urn, and flanked by Mary Frances and the mayor, was the center of attention.

When Kate looked again, Timmy was gone.

"So will you join us?" Joe was speaking to

her. She steeled herself, trying to focus. Obviously, he'd just asked her a question, but she'd been concentrating on Marlene, who seemed to be sleepwalking her way back to the pool area.

"Join you . . . where?"

"On the sailboat." Joe sounded annoyed or puzzled. What was he talking about? "After the reception, I'd like you ladies to be part of Stella's final voyage."

"We'll need to wear deck shoes and change our clothes," Mary Frances said. "And I want to get out of this black dress. I don't think we should go sailing looking like we're at a funeral."

Marlene stepped back into the group. "Of course, Joe, we all want to say a last good-bye to Stella."

The mayor said, "I'm so sorry, I can't come. I'm heading back to Town Hall now."

Kate thought Brenda Walters didn't look quite as attractive in the bright sunlight, but then who did? Every pore showed. And makeup that flattered indoors often turned garish in the cruel light of day. The mayor had tiny white lines around her temples. Face-lift scars. Unlike old soldiers, those scars fade but they never go away.

"However, I'd like all of you to be my guests tonight at the Broward County Main Library. It's the kickoff cocktail party for the Book Bash. Dave Barry will be there. And the governor." She paused, then patted Joe's arm. "This is such a sad day, but I believe Stella would want you to join me tonight."

Now that was one event Kate didn't want to miss. But first, she wanted to get her hands on the elusive yearbook and ask her sister-in-law a few questions.

The recreation room's glass door slid open and the large square-jawed caterer announced, "Soup's on!" Stella's mourners formed a double line and moved back inside.

The table that had held the old photographs and the yearbook now boasted a lazy Susan filled with crudités and various salad dressings.

Don't panic, she told herself, then did. Yet . . . the caterers or the undertakers had to have stashed the photos and the yearbook somewhere nearby, right? She sought out Samuel Adams, who was directing traffic to and from the kitchen.

"Where's Stella's yearbook?" Kate could hear her high-pitched anxiety. She pointed. "It was on the table over there."

Adams kept moving. "I carefully packed away those photographs myself. They're in a box to the right of the lobby door. I didn't see the yearbook. Mr. Sajak must have it."

"He only has the urn," Kate said, her voice catching.

"Well, maybe someone is holding the yearbook for him." Adams picked up speed, indicating he thought this conversation was over.

An upset Joe Sajak assured Kate he hadn't assigned the yearbook's safekeeping to anyone else, then angrily ordered the caterers to go through every box and to empty every trash bag.

And where the devil had Marlene gone? Apparently, she hadn't come back inside for the reception.

An hour later when Mary Frances, Joe, and Kate left the reception to change their clothes and get ready to head down to Pier 66, no one had found the yearbook.

Kate, who'd been helping Joe search, finally accepted that her sister-in-law, like the yearbook, had vanished.

They arrived at Pier 66 minus Marlene. She'd called Joe Sajak from God knows where, explaining that something had come up and she was sorry to have missed the reception, but she would arrive at Pier 66 by one-fifteen, their estimated time of departure.

So now they were three, Joe in the lead, clutching the urn.

The Pier 66 Hotel and Marina, a Fort Lauderdale landmark, wore its age well.

Motor yachts, sloops, trawlers, cigarette boats, and houseboats were among the many craft berthed at its docks. Under a brilliant blue sky and enough breeze to temper the sunshine, the Atlantic Ocean fore and the Intercoastal aft, the setting was beyond beautiful.

"Is that Travis McGee's slip?" Mary Frances asked.

Kate, a great fan of John MacDonald's, smiled. "According to the marker, it is. I always pictured the houseboat over there." Kate pointed slightly to the west. Though usually delighted to discuss her favorite mystery authors and their characters, this afternoon Kate was too puzzled about Marlene's strange behavior to enjoy chatting about Travis McGee.

Joe looked at his watch. "One-fifteen. Let's board."

Mary Frances untied the lines.

At Kate's look of surprise, she said, "I took a Coast Guard course just as soon as I moved to South Florida." Her green eyes, twinkling in the sunshine, locked onto Joe's. "You never know when you'll meet a sailor, do you?"

Kate came aboard, and Joe hoisted the main as Mary Frances was casting off the last rope.

"Ahoy! I'm here." Marlene had arrived.

Sailing out to sea, they passed some of the most expensive real estate in the world: mansion after mansion with Shannon green lawns and elaborate docks housing sleek white yachts. Joe was a good captain and the thirty-foot Catalina seemed easy to handle. Marlene, still dressed in the caftan that she'd worn to the memorial, was barefoot, her sandals stowed under a seat in the cabin. Kate sat across the deck from Marlene, holding the Persian urn. She hoped it would be a smooth voyage.

With Mary Frances at the wheel and Joe busy with the sails, Kate said, "Where were you, Marlene? I saw you with Timmy, then you disappeared."

"Lower your voice," Marlene snapped. "You sound like I've committed a crime."

Kate thought, Well, have you?

"For your information, I was with Detective Carbone. I'd told Timmy to meet me at my car. I didn't want him going to the police alone."

Stunned, Kate asked, "What happened?"

"Timmy ran away because he was frightened and felt guilty. He'd delivered a note to Stella, then she was murdered. He figured there had to be a connection. Yesterday afternoon, he'd tried to contact me to ask what he should do. When he couldn't reach me, he called Oberon, who lived in Del Ray, and who showed up at the phone booth while Timmy was waiting for me to return his call. When he saw you and Mary Frances, he panicked and ran away . . . again. Then today he read that Oberon had committed suicide and he came looking for me."

"Panic can make us do strange things," Kate said. "Does Timmy think Oberon was working alone?"

Marlene shook her head. "Wyndam Oberon

had been talking to someone on his cell phone when Timmy met him Tuesday on the pier. And he overheard Oberon say, 'Timmy's here now.' "

The ocean was choppier than Kate had hoped. She'd sailed aboard a good number of boats, but had never been part of a burial at sea. When Joe dropped anchor, she clutched the urn with both hands. Joe gently took it from her and they all stood starboard, the wind to their backs. He opened the urn and held it at arm's length over the rail, then turned it upside down. "Good-bye, Stella Maris, my star of the sea." The ashes didn't really scatter, but rather drifted over the water, like sand in the wind.

As they sailed back in silence, Kate felt compelled to break it. She had to know. "Joe, how did Martin Baum commit suicide?"

Sajak looked angry. Because she'd broken the silence? Or because she'd asked that question? "He shot himself through the head." Joe sounded flat. His baritone dulled.

"Did anyone ever think it might not have been suicide?"

Joe stared at her. "Only Stella. At first, she talked about 'her theory' a lot, but then she seemed to forget all about it." He sighed. "The man killed himself, Kate. You should forget about it, too."

THIRTY

One of the reasons Kate had acquiesced to living in South Florida was the Best Library in the United States Award–winning Broward County Main Library. Located just off Broward Boulevard in downtown Fort Lauderdale, the library was big, beautiful, modern, and user friendly.

As Kate rode the escalator up to the second-floor cocktail party, she admired its clean lines and cool architecture. Maybe she'd volunteer to spend some time here . . . if Jeff Stein didn't offer her a position at the *Palmetto Beach Gazette*. God, what was she thinking?

At least that thought took her mind off murder, albeit temporarily.

Marlene poked her. "We're here. Stop day-dreaming and step off."

The wide-open space was packed with literary types, their readers, and their wealthy bene-factors — the latter two not necessarily being mutually exclusive. Some of South Florida's millionaires enjoyed having a reading room or a center with their name on a bronze plaque above the door, even if that plaque would be the only item they'd ever read.

The mayor, wearing a narrow black jersey dress and looking as modern and beautiful as the library's design, greeted Kate and Marlene like old friends.

Kate in a blue silk pants suit, one of Charlie's favorites, suddenly felt frumpy. Marlene wore an orange and yellow print that Kate had considered relatively subdued, but now seemed flashy.

Joe and Mary Frances, who'd been talking nonstop since they left Ocean Vista in Marlene's convertible, joined them. As the mayor took Joe's right hand in both of hers, she said, "I'm so pleased you came. Let me get you a drink."

"I can't get over how much you remind me of someone," Joe said, "an actress or —"

"Oh, Joe, you flatterer, I'm only Brenda Walters."

At that instant, Kate's lost memory hidden behind a senior moment broke out, coming through loud and clear.

"Excuse me," she said, "there's something I have to do." She left the quartet debating what they wanted to drink, and headed around the corner and up the stairs to a bank of computers.

Within a few minutes, she'd brought up BEDFORD FALLS HIGH SCHOOL, clicked on 1958, and scrolled down to YEARBOOK. She entered SCIENCE HONORS, and up popped the page with the photograph of Martin

Baum and his four honor students.

She zeroed in on the girl with the bumpy nose. Yes! The same eyes, the same heart-shaped face, but in addition to a face-lift, the mayor also had had a nose job. Just as the Pekinese Samantha had become Serendipity, Bea Wernoski had become Brenda Walters and, like so many other name changers, had kept the same initials.

Reveling in her recently restored memory, Kate pictured Stella starting to introduce the mayor as "Bea," stumbling for a second, then quickly switching to Brenda.

"Kate." The well-modulated voice caught her off guard. She looked up from the heart-shaped face in the old photograph into the heart-shaped face of Mayor Brenda Walters.

"I'm so sorry, Ballou, we're going out right now!"

Still dressed in her blue pants suit, Kate struggled to get the leash on an indignant, yelping, overexcited Ballou. With today's jam-packed schedule focused on mourning, murder, and the mayor, her poor dog hadn't been walked since this morning. How could she have been so cruel to the animal she loved?

She'd take Ballou out, talk over her theory with Marlene — who'd agreed to meet her on the beach — then call Carbone. But what if she was dead wrong? After all, her case against the mayor was circumstantial at best. Not a shred of proof other than Stella having said "Bea" instead of Brenda, and the mayor having the same heart-shaped face and the same initials as the teenage Bea Wernoski.

The mayor had been both charming and chatty when Kate had looked up from the computer and into her smiling heart-shaped face. If Brenda Walters had caught a glimpse of the Science Club photograph, she certainly gave no indication of anger, or fear, or even concern. She'd only asked what Kate would like to drink. No wonder Kate was questioning her own thought processes. Still . . . Charlie's heaven-sent clue and her own now crystal-clear memory of Stella's slip of the tongue seemed to confirm her theory. And Wyndam Oberon's "suicide" seemed to be a copycat of Martin Baum's.

Of course, she hadn't been able to discuss a word of this turmoil with Marlene because Mary Frances and Joe had been in tow.

"Come on, Ballou, let's go confer with Auntie Marlene."

Though it was only eight o'clock, the beach was deserted and dark. Since she usually walked Ballou earlier, Kate hadn't realized how much darker these early November evenings had become. And with the moon and the stars almost hidden behind clouds in an overcast sky, there appeared to be eerie shadows stalking her in the sand.

Where *was* Marlene? Kate had no choice; Ballou had to go. Now. With her pooper-scooper at the ready, they headed north toward the pier. Maybe Marlene was on the phone with Detective Carbone, making sure that Timmy faced no charges. She'd show up. Soon, Kate hoped.

A fog horn sounded in the distance. A boat heading to Port Everglades. Had Stella's ashes settled into the sea? Into a watery grave. Were the dead lonely? Kate decided that she'd go to the cemetery tomorrow and visit Charlie.

A sharp blow to her head, followed by a powerful shove into the ocean, brought Kate to her knees. As she fought to stand, a wave knocked her down, and she tasted saltwater mixed with blood. She could hear Ballou barking. Strange, he sounded so sad. Then two hands were on her shoulders, pushing her under. She landed face first on the ocean bottom. With sand in her teeth and terror in her heart, she regained her footing and thrust herself upward, gasping for air, only to be struck a second time. Her head pounding, Kate slipped under again, certain she was drowning. Ballou's barking had faded away.

THIRTY-ONE

A squeeze of her hand, a lick on her right cheek, and the sound of Dean Martin singing *"Everybody loves somebody sometime"* woke Kate up.

She was afraid to open her eyes. Could she be in heaven? Could that be Charlie squeezing her hand? Even if the answers to those questions were yes, Kate wanted to be alive. Prayed to be alive. Her head hurt like hell. Good: The dead felt no pain.

She slowly opened her eyes and, without moving, looked around. Marlene sat on one side of her bed; Joe, holding Ballou, sat on the other.

"Where am I?"

"Imperial Point Hospital ER." Marlene stood and came over to Kate, planting a kiss on her other cheek. "You swallowed a lot of ocean and you have two nasty head wounds, one causing a concussion, but you're going to be okay."

"What happened?"

"Ballou's a hero, Kate." Marlene smiled. "He barked and yelped under my balcony until I hung up on Carbone. When I saw how agitated Ballou was, I jumped off the balcony — good thing it's only two feet off the sand — and followed him down to the ocean."

"Marlene saved your life, Kate," Joe said. "She punched the mayor, breaking her nose, then dove into the ocean and pulled you out."

Kate's eyes filled with tears. "Thank you, Marlene. Thank you, Ballou."

"Yes," Joe said as the dog struggled to get closer to Kate, "you're quite the detective, Kate Kennedy."

"Brenda Walters has confessed." Marlene walked around the bed and took the Westie from Joe. "Stella recognized Brenda and was blackmailing her. The two hundred thousand dollars was to be the first of two payments. Seems that Stella had witnessed Bea Wernoski murder Martin Baum all those decades ago and had never told the Bedford Falls Police."

Kate started, then tried to sit up. A sharp pain stampeded through her brain. She returned her head to the pillow. "Why hadn't Stella told the police?"

Joe sighed. "It seems you were right on all counts, Kate. According to Bea Wernoski, Stella had been involved with Martin Baum, too. I guess Stella thought he got what he deserved."

"Who knows?" Marlene said. "Maybe Stella had planned to blackmail Bea all along, but

Bea skipped town right after graduation."

"And Nancy Cooper found the connection?" Kate wondered how.

Marlene nodded, "Yes. Stella may or may not have visited her Tuesday afternoon, but after Stella's murder, Nancy discovered a photocopy of the cashier's check while rereading her copious obituary notes. Stella had printed *B.W.* on the photocopy and the words *first payment*. When Nancy Cooper questioned the mayor for her big story, Brenda Walters had to kill her, too."

"Then tried to get rid of me." Kate felt cold. "I guess Nancy's last word was *Oh* as in surprise, not *O* as in Oberon."

"Right," Marlene said. "And when the attorney panicked, the mayor staged her second suicide, putting the murder weapon in his hand."

Marlene put Ballou on the bed. The little dog gently snuggled against Kate's side.

EPILOGUE

Marlene's act of heroism eased, but didn't erase the guilt of her long-ago adultery with Charlie: a four-martini one-night stand.

Putting on a mitt, she took Kate's favorite baked ziti out of the oven. The reorganized Hearts club — Marlene, Mary Frances, Joe, and Kate — would be playing together for the first time tonight.

Marlene sighed and decided to deal with her guilt the same way she dealt with the Queen of Spades when she couldn't discard it: She'd just have to live with it.

The employees of Thorndike Press hope you have enjoyed this Large Print book. All our Thorndike and Wheeler Large Print titles are designed for easy reading, and all our books are made to last. Other Thorndike Press Large Print books are available at your library, through selected bookstores, or directly from us.

For information about titles, please call:

(800) 223-1244

or visit our Web site at:

www.gale.com/thorndike
www.gale.com/wheeler

To share your comments, please write:

Publisher
Thorndike Press
295 Kennedy Memorial Drive
Waterville, ME   04901